STALLION OF THE SANDS

The beautiful white stallion was a throw-back to the horses taken to South America by the Spaniards in the sixteenth century. It had narrowly escaped being captured by the gauchos, and had been forced to take refuge miles from its homeland plains—in the barren coastal lands. Now it had become a legend: a ghostly shape in the sea mists on those wild Atlantic shores. It was said that the man who succeeded in capturing and riding the sand stallion would be the most gaucho of all of them.

For Aurelio, an orphan who dreamed of being accepted as a gaucho by his companions, the challenge was too strong to resist. In his quest for the elusive animal, he solved the mystery of what had brought him to the pampa in the first place. And the lonely stallion learned through his gentleness that not all mankind was to be feared, and that there was more than one kind of freedom.

Jacket illustration by Edwin Philips

HELEN GRIFFITHS

Stallion of the Sands

Illustrated by Victor G. Ambrus

KNIGHT BOOKS
Hodder and Stoughton

© Helen Griffiths 1968
Illustration © Hutchinson Junior
Books Ltd 1968

First published in Knight Books 1978

———————————————

Printed and bound in Great Britain for
Hodder and Stoughton Paperbacks, a
division of Hodder and Stoughton Ltd.,
Mill Road, Dunton Green, Sevenoaks,
Kent (Editorial Office: 47 Bedford
Square, London, WC1 3DP) by
Richard Clay (The Chaucer Press) Ltd
Bungay, Suffolk

ISBN 0 340 21383 3

Contents

1 : The foal

On a bright day in early spring the albino colt was born.
There was nothing to differentiate him from the other
half a dozen colts born during the same day except his
colouring. The others were bays and duns with frizzy
black tails and manes and perhaps a white splash on the

face or leg; there were two red-and-white foals with hides dappled like cloud shadows on the grass; but only he was the colour of the spring cloud itself, touched with the pink of sunset.

Snow white was his woolly tail and brushy mane; snow white the fluffy hair that thickly covered him. And pink were his lips and nostrils and all his flesh, and the eyes that opened wonderingly.

In everything else he was like the others, a gangling bundle of bone and damp skin at birth, shivering on the soft earth while his mother pummelled warmth into him with soft and busy muzzle. The light and the air and the scents all about him were overwhelming in the first seconds of his life and he clung to the earth, stiff and trembling, until warm blood began to pulse through his veins, the clouds faded from his eyes, and his lungs took on an even rhythm.

Then the air was no longer a cold force, crushing him, and the light no longer hurt or bewildered him. His stiff legs began to kick, his big ungainly head to twist about. Within seconds he was lying upright, his legs more or less gathered under him, and for the first time he was taking a look at the world.

All he could see was grass and the long solid legs of his mother. He could smell the freshness of the grass and he could smell the warm, sweaty scent of his mother. He knew instinctively that she was his dam, his strength, the key to his existence, and his first outstretchings were towards her. The pink muzzle touched at her legs, wrinkling as it did so, and the mare's head came close, big and comforting.

She whickered softly and the colt grunted in answer, moving his head convulsively in his first efforts to rise to all fours. Strength began to surge into his forequarters. There was an urge to push, push upwards, raise himself from the ground. As the strength coursed through all his body the urge grew stronger and the colt grunted and struggled and collapsed until within seconds, and almost without realising how it was done, he was on his legs; legs that stuck out like four ungainly poles, wobbling, unsteady; and he, supported by them, afraid to move.

The mare rubbed her head against the foal's withers and he collapsed. But soon he was up again, his legs better gathered the second time, though still he staggered and was stiff with uncertainty. After a second tumble he suddenly understood the idea and the third time that he was up on his legs he was there to stay. His mother pushed and nibbled and licked at rough patches but he was strong enough to resist her movements and not be tumbled by them.

Soon he was moving about her, his legs going like those of a marionette. Within minutes he was prancing, tossing his large white head, flicking his brushy tail. All stiffness, all strangeness, was gone. He could walk and twist and dance and his legs were part of him instead of the props that they had earlier been.

He sniffed the earth and the grass and the warm body of his dam, and the latter was the only one that attracted him or held meaning for him. The sensitive lips twitched along her body, from breast to flank, from flank to belly, searching, searching. . . . Hardly knowing for what they searched until they discovered the udder with its life-giving milk, hot and rich.

The foal clung excitedly, his whole white body aquiver, tail flicking, ears twitching, legs stamping, and he drank until his belly could hold no more, until he was swollen and uncomfortable; and then the lips relaxed their hold, the pink eyes drooped, and his body slipped into delicious unconsciousness, tumbled on the ground beside his mother.

The mare lowered her head and passed her lips across his soft back and swollen flank. Then she began to pull hungrily at the grass, moving in a small circle about the sleeping colt. She seemed unaware of his existence while she grazed; not once did she lift her head to glance at him or flick an ear in his direction, but not for a moment did her shadow cease to fall very close to him.

II

For the first few days there was little in the colt's life but this, sucking at his dam, practising a gambol or so and sleeping almost unconsciously. He was still hardly aware of the great herd to which he and his mother belonged. Its members grazed in a scattered fashion and there was not another horse within half a mile of his mother's grazing. He was hardly aware of the rising of the sun or of its setting, so distant was everything from his understanding. He felt the sun's warmth on his back and it pleased him; he felt the playful breeze that tugged at his tail, tickling him and making him dance on his yellow, rubbery hooves, but when the sky grew dark and his mother a dark shadow with it, he did not know that it was because the sun had gone.

For the first few days his world began and ended with the mother horse. The grass under his hooves, the birds that sang in the grasses by day and screeched blood-curdlingly at night, the sun and the breeze, all were things that held no meaning for him.

On the fourth day of his life, however, various incidents occurred which woke him to the fact that his mother was not the only being in existence besides himself and that if he used his eyes and his nose and his ears he would grow aware of many things more. It was the day that his mother decided to introduce him to the herd.

On that day she did not fall to grazing as was her custom but instead set off in the direction of her companions. The colt had never seen her move with such determination and he stood staring at her for several minutes, ears pricked, bewildered in expression, as she drew further and further away from him. He bleated after her anxiously and stamped a hoof. The mare halted and looked back, whickering to her youngling, telling him to follow. Then she continued on her way.

The colt was angry now. He stamped again, flattened his ears and made his first attempt to whinny. The sound came out in a broken squeal and he shook his head in surprise, but the mare refused to look back, expecting the colt to obey. He squealed again, stretching out his neck to give more force to the call, and turned angrily from left to right, still stamping and flicking his tail.

The mare stopped, turned her head to stare back at the colt with patient eyes, whinnied once more and waited. But when the colt still refused to come, she resumed her walk, ignoring him. The foal lost his righteous anger. His haughty impatience deserted him. He was a baby again whose mother was almost far away. He was suddenly afraid and, making up his mind with one last shake of his head, he sprang stiffly into the air then raced after her. His long white legs swept over the grass gracefully and the breeze grew into a wind as he ran against it, blowing into his eyes and ears and against his neck.

He discovered that there was a joy in running, in feeling the soft turf spring under his hooves. As he neared his dam and his fear disappeared he began to kick and buck and prance in sheer delight, his pink nostrils stretched wide to breathe in the air that was suddenly nectar, and his eyes were bright with joy.

He reached his dam and did not want to stop. He circled about her, racing still, lowering his head between his front legs to buck, but the mare hardly glanced at him, used to the ways of foals.

The colt wanted her to notice him. He grew wilder in his game, kicking, tossing, gambolling about her. Suddenly his legs knotted themselves over a tuft of thick grass and he sprawled to the ground with a thud. A breathless bleat of surprise was knocked out of him and for a moment he lay in a tumbled heap, the sky and the grass swirling about him, making him dizzy. He scrambled up but he had learnt his lesson and when once again his mother called him he was content to trot along at her side, his muzzle touching her flank, in the sedate manner that all good foals should employ.

They had not gone far when the foal became aware of a new scent assailing his nostrils. His nose twitched and his ears strained eagerly forward. He was aware too of his mother's excitement and halted when she halted, clinging close to her, almost afraid of this new thing that was happening to him.

There were horses, many horses, none of them far away, and the colt could see as well as smell them. They hardly moved, for most of them were busy grazing and the foal could hear the champing of their jaws and the occasional hoof stamping.

He was startled by the loud neigh suddenly uttered by

his mother and flattened his ears. Simultaneously most of the horses of the herd stopped their grazing and looked up, ears pricked, in the direction of the mare and the white foal. They stared for a few seconds, one or two whickered a greeting in return, and then they dropped their heads again and continued to tear at the grass.

When some seconds had passed the mare, now sure of her welcome, resumed her walk towards the herd but she had hardly taken more than a few paces when one of its members broke away from the main bunch and came towards her. It was a yearling colt, with gleaming red patches on a white coat, and he came towards the lone pair at a fast canter, skidding to a halt just a yard or two away, tossing his head and whickering deeply in his throat.

The mare and the yearling stared at each other, the former unperturbed but the latter very much agitated. He pranced on the spot for a moment or two then drew closer, hesitatingly, as if unsure of the reception he would be given. The mare tossed her head and slightly changed her direction, moving away from him, but the foal, greatly impressed by the newcomer, stood his ground and watched in fascination.

The yearling did not see the foal. He went after the mare, tail swishing, grunting anxiously, trying to push himself under her head. She shied away, nipping at the colt with her teeth, and when he came after her again she lunged at him in true anger, ripping this time and flattening her ears. The colt squealed, backed away, but again he returned to her, not understanding. This was his mother, at whose side he had run for the whole of a year. That she no longer wanted him was beyond his understanding.

The mare quickly wearied of the importunate animal. All her patience was now for the new foal that followed at her heels. This one she no longer recognised as her youngling. As he came up to her, cowed and pleading, she thrashed at him with her hooves, buffeting him heavily in the ribs and the colt almost lost his balance as he staggered away. He nearly fell over the albino colt, his brother, and lunged at the slender creature in his anger.

The mother squealed and came after the yearling again but the latter knew when he was beaten and he dashed back to the herd, aware at last that she had forsaken him. The mare caressed the foal with a movement of her head, and then she followed the colt, insisting that her youngling stick close beside her.

Soon he and the mare had horses on all sides of them and the foal was afraid of so many of his kind, all towering over him, sniffing at him, nibbling at him before turning away. The mare watched over him carefully to see that none treated him badly in his first contact with them. He cringed against her flank, his eyes big and white ringed as they stared upon so many curious muzzles that poked at him, and his heart beat painfully against his ribs, fast in fear.

His mother seemed on equal terms with all of them and was afraid of none. She pushed away curious yearlings but welcomed the greetings of her companions and just as the foal was growing accustomed to the bewildering number of mares that prodded him harmlessly they all drew aside to make way for the approach of a horse, bigger and more powerful than any of them and of which all seemed to be slightly afraid. It was the stallion, the lord of the herd, the sire of the albino foal.

He was not the most beautiful of animals for he had

dwelt some twenty years on the pampa and had fought many battles. His ears were almost gone, chewn to nothing by his rivals; a great gash scarred all one side of his head and the eye was withered to a half closed socket. His whole body was marked with clefts torn by the hooves of his challengers and only at nightfall, when darkness hid the ugliness, was there a certain beauty in the carriage of his heavily maned head, the haughtiness of his stance, the thickness of his muscles.

He was a grey roan, but twenty winters had whitened the greyness and he was almost as white as his albino offspring. The one eye left to him was bold and glittering and wild, and the other mares drew away as he approached the albino's dam, snorting, tossing his head, prancing heavily.

She timidly awaited him, accepting the rough caresses he gave her in welcome, hardly moving as he circled about her, sniffing her flanks and back and belly and legs, grunting all the while. The foal was really afraid of this all powerful being and backed hurriedly away as at last the stallion's attention was drawn to his newest offspring and he drew close to sniff at him.

But it was only cursory attention. His interest was in the mare and he circled constantly about her, ignoring all the others in the herd, while she occasionally returned his attentions and sometimes pulled at the grass.

2 : Grass and sunshine

The albino foal grew rapidly. For all that he continued to gain his daily sustenance from the mare and sought her protection whenever there was anything to frighten or disturb him, a sense of independence drew him gradually further and further from her. The whole of the pampa was his playground, flat, vast, unending, and there were many things to discover, many things to see and smell, many things to enjoy.

Firstly there were the other foals, some older, some younger than himself, and all with his same desire to play and explore. Most of the mothers drew by seemingly common consent into a big circle and within the bounds of this circle the young colts and fillies played. They raced about with tossing heads and flying hooves; they fought mock battles with each other, the colt foals born with the instinct to bluff with abrupt rearings and stamping hooves, and the fillies watched them with curiosity, as one day they might watch real stallions fight for possession of them.

When they tired of running and bucking and squealing they would throw themselves down in twos or threes, keeping the flies from each other with constantly flicking tails. They nibbled at each other's foreheads or necks or withers and occasionally carried on a conversation of short grunts, nickers and small squeals, or touched noses when they were too hot or too tired for more energetic exchanges.

But the foals were not always in this common nursery. For all that the herd was more or less static, living within the bounds of the grass and herbs that grew abundantly about them, there were times when a general consent to move came over them and they would march at a grazing pace to new pastures. Then the albino might lose sight of his fellows for several days, for the herd moved in a scattered fashion, covering three or four miles from its tip to its tail. Sometimes the albino and his mother would be close to ten or twenty others and sometimes almost completely alone.

The albino would grow impatient with his mother's slow pace, hardly moving two strides in five minutes. He wanted to race and rear and chase the shadows and he would wander off on his own to explore, never very far, always within sight or calling distance of his dam, but far enough for him to feel bold and almost frightened.

It was on these excursions of his own that he grew aware of most of the other pampa dwellers. Following a strange scent that might lead to a thicket of plumy grass, he would come across a nesting bird which would fly up under his nose in fearful surprise, frightening him and sending him cavorting away with snorts and flattened ears. There were many birds that nested in the grass but most of them nested in big communities so that at the approach of the horses they would rise up with madly flapping wings and screeching voices. The horses would shy away from them, startled, and thus avoid crushing the nests.

On one occasion the albino met an armadillo, a creature which attracted him by its strangeness and the unconcerned way in which it continued its journey unafraid of the pink damp nose suddenly prodding at it. It waddled on, perhaps just a little faster as the colt began pushing at it with his muzzle, but the albino was not satisfied with just a sniff or so and suddenly tried pawing at it with his hoof. Then the armadillo decided that it was time to move more rapidly and, in spite of its ungainly appearance and former plodding gait, it suddenly shot ahead with astonishing rapidity, downed its nose into the earth and began a furious digging.

The colt drew closer, ears pricked, eyes bright with interest, but every time he dropped his head to sniff at the strange discovery the armadillo showered him with earth that sprayed out from its back legs, keeping him at bay. Within seconds the armadillo was inside the hole he had dug himself. Only his tail was visible and that too, with one last flick, suddenly disappeared. The colt was left with a narrow hole of softly falling earth and a scent that lingered for a few moments to puzzle him.

Another time the foal spied not far off a group of pampa deer. From a distance they did not seem unlike his play-fellows. There was no scent, for the breeze blew against him, and with sudden joy he set off at a skittish canter towards them. But then the breeze changed direction and the albino drew to a startled halt. The scent of the pretty fawn-coloured creatures was so repugnant that even curiosity would not draw him closer. He squealed and kicked and shook his head then turned and galloped back to his dam and for all that he was to meet the harmless deer on many future occasions he could never abide the smell of them and always gave them a wide berth.

The spring passed and half the summer. The albino foal and his fellows learned in this time what they might expect to meet and smell and hear. The night noises that had at first startled and even frightened them—the booming of the vizcachas, furry rodents that came up noisily from their burrows when the sun was gone; the squeals and whispers of squabbling, food-hunting rats; the wild screechings and sobbing cries of the different birds—were by now a customary harmony without which they would probably rest uneasily.

There even came a time when the foal lost interest in his neighbours, so accustomed to them did he grow. The most common of them were the huge rheas and the guanacos that mingled with them. The rheas lived in communities as large as those of the horses and often the two grazed side by side, keeping apace with each other though never intermingling. The rhea was the cleverest creature on the pampa, cunning, quick-witted, as swift or even swifter than the horses, and it would seem that the guanaco sensed this for the latter had almost no sense at all and was entirely defenceless against any would-be enemy.

The rhea and the guanaco shared the same tall necks and haughty, rather silly-looking faces; there was even a similarity in the woolly-looking feathers of the former, drooping from their backs like grey moss, and the shaggy drooping coats of the latter. Both had thickly covered backs and almost naked underparts, both had long legs. One was bird and the other mammal but they lived in harmony and the guanaco had little need to fear with the rhea to protect him.

II

Until the approach of midsummer the weather had been benign with the young colt, the sky an arc of blue, tossed with clouds as white as himself, the earth yielding to his tender hooves, ever sprouting grass and flowers to make his soft and sweet-smelling bed. But gradually the clouds disappeared from the sky and every day dawned with a heat more intense than its predecessors. The sky was blue, deeply, scorchingly blue, and the only thing to break its blueness was the glittering blaze of silver sun which became unbearable as the day advanced. When such blueness came to the sky, and the sun turned silver in its heat, the grass and the flowers withered and the earth grew hard.

It hurt the colt's hooves to gallop over that summer earth which was now brown and cracked and moisture-less. The sun that had glowed so pleasantly upon his rump now burnt him and seemed to burrow into his very depths, drawing out every drop of energy and leaving him as sapless as the grass. In such heat all the horses stood listless. They had not even the energy to graze, nor little appetite for what they found. Lips swollen with thirst, they pulled at the desiccated grass and when they stamped a hoof to rid themselves of the flies that endlessly bit at their legs they raised a cloud of fine dust about them.

They passed half the day kicking up dust over their bellies and some even rolled in it, desperate with the flies that tormented them, the only beings seemingly unaffected by the racking heat. The foals watched their mothers and followed the set example. They rolled in the dust but there was little joy in their rolling for they were as languid as their dams.

When dusk fell the earth seemed to stretch a little, released from its long hours of torture. The horses grazed with more animation although the grass they found was tasteless. The foals sucked at their dams with greater eagerness, overcome with appetite in the cool darkness, and the mares were not so irritated by them as during the day.

At dusk the herd began to move. It moved of one accord, travelling fairly swiftly in comparison with its usual nonchalant gait, for all its members were of one intention. They needed water; water to drink, water to wallow in; the cool contact of mud and rushes. During the day the heat filled them with inertia and they stood or lay unmoving, almost like a herd of phantom horses against a shimmering, phantom scenery.

It took four nights of travel to reach the water nearest to them. As they drew close they could smell it in the air,

sweet and tempting, and the almost silent herd grew noisy
with restless anticipatory whickers and grunts. They
came upon it just before sunrise, a sullen, marshy river
that had shrunk to a trickle surrounded by mud. But the
trickle continued undaunted until it reached its destination, the mouth of a once wide lake whose shores were
thick with bullrushes, hock-high grass, fragrant herbs and
flowers.

The mares and fillies, the colts, young stallions and
foals, more than eight hundred in all, strung themselves
out along the banks of the river and around the lake.
The impatient ones pushed against each other, bit and
kicked for a place; round the lake they sank up to their
bellies in mud and water weeds. They whinnied and
tossed their shaggy heads, they thrashed out and com-
plained, but as the sun climbed high above them, dis-
pelling the gloom of the night with its golden brightness,
every horse had found a drinking place and most of them
had their heads bent gratefully to the water and were
sucking slowly with parched lips.

As their thirst was satiated they returned to the solid
banks. They grazed in the grass, still luscious at this place;
they chewed the heads off the flowers; they hid themselves
in the dark green rushes and protected themselves from
the sun.

At the rising of the sun the lake became inhabited by
more and more occupants. The horses retreated and at
their clumsy retreat the wild duck fled out from their
shelter among the rushes, gliding down in the centre of
the water with loud squawks and a great fluster of wings.
Herons and spoonbills stalked with less flurry and more
grace across the dried mud flats, delicately paused for a
second before continuing through the wet black mud down

to the shrinking water's edge, and dipped their bills to gather up the first moisture of the day. The waders ignored the horses and the horses seemed unaware of them.

The leader of the herd, the half-blind stallion, was one of the last to desert the water. He had waded into the lake until it almost covered him and he stood there, immobile, soaking his scarred old body in its coolness, the ends of his thick mane touching the water. His favourite mare stood at a little distance from him. The water came up to her hocks but she would venture no closer to the stallion.

All about the shores of the lake there were horses bathing thus. They caked themselves up to their bellies with mud and the flies could not bite at them.

The albino colt had followed his mother to the water. By the time they reached it, it was murky and hardly appetising, stirred up by so many bodies and legs. But the mare drank gratefully and the colt nibbled at the wavelets also. He liked the feel of the cool wetness about him and waded up to his withers, safe while he could feel the ground beneath his hooves.

When he was still he could see his reflection in the water. It puzzled him, that other white head with pricked ears and pink, white-whiskered muzzle, and when he reached down his nose to sniff at the newcomer, he jumped with surprise as the water flooded his nostrils.

He lost his balance, struggled to regain it and failed. The water shot up on every side of him, the ducks flew up of one accord with loud shrieks, the stallion in four great bounds was on solid land, his favourite mare beside him, and even the waders held their narrow heads high and looked startled. Meanwhile, the albino foal thrashed about in the water while his dam uttered anxious whinnies from the bank until he found land under his hooves again and raised himself dripping from the mire he had stirred up on every side.

Bedraggled and streaked with black mud, the foal staggered to the protection of his dam, snorting and gasping and shaking his waterlogged head. Weeds clung round his ears and legs and dangled from his tail. He stood on the bank and trembled while his mother nuzzled comfort into him and then he followed her meekly to a sheltered spot among the rushes, far enough from the water for him to forget his fear of it.

He burrowed into the cool green shade of the rushes and gradually the mud dried over him and clung to his hair. By late afternoon the adventure was forgotten.

He came down to the edge of the lake again, this time not venturing to wet himself, but he stood in the soft mud for a long time watching the birds with pricked ears and bright eyes. The sun was glowing on the water, making golden ripples in its greyness. The ducks were still squabbling and chasing about noisily.

A sudden shaking of wings drew the colt's attention to the farther side of the lake and there he saw two birds that he had not seen before. White and rose-coloured were they and crimson were the undersides of their wings. It looked as though the sun had caught them in its glow, filling them with the colour of sunset. The colt's eyes glowed with the same colour as he stared at the flamingos.

3 : Yearling

The summer passed and with its passing half of the albino foal's babyhood was gone. He had grown a lot in six months and was now a sturdy-looking creature. He had thrown off the almost comical innocence expressed in nearly every movement of his gangling, baby body and his pricked ears, wide-breathing nostrils and intelligent eyes gave him closer affinity to the future than to the past.

His slender legs were passing gradually from the gambolling, frisky stage and developing a movement that was extravagant in its showiness and gave haughtiness to his stride. He cantered now, rather than frisked, and with his long arched neck, proud Roman features, silky mane and tail, there was a natural beauty about him that many of his companions lacked. He was as strong and long-bodied as they were but with greater elegance and promising greater stature. In all he gave signs that he was a throwback to the Jennets with their oriental blood which the Spaniards first brought to the land. It was blood which still coursed strongly through all the criollo ponies although its dominant features were mainly lost through the natural selection forced upon them in their unhampered wanderings.

In the herd to which the albino belonged there were perhaps fifty horses as beautiful as he was destined to become, among them greys with black points, bays and most of the roans. There was a nobility in their expression, in the carriage of their heads and their graceful movements that all their wildness could never deny. The albino possessed this same nobility and, as his foalhood gradually faded, so it began to show.

With the coming of autumn began the best time of all for the colt. The molesting summer heat was gone and there were showers which refreshed both animals and plants alike. The ground grew soft and resilient again, perfect for prancing over, and began to sprout the first green blades of winter grass at which the horses tugged with so much eagerness.

The colt, too, was tempted to browse among such

tender shoots and their sweetness soon had him pulling and searching with as much voraciousness as his mother. He still came to her for the bulk of his sustenance but she began to push him aside with greater impatience, swinging her hindquarters in his path or crossly kicking whenever his head came searching under her belly. After a while the colt decided that the grass was as sweet as milk to him and no longer demanded insistently as in foalhood.

He was often hungry at first and lost some of his tubbiness. He had to roam for his food and had less time to gambol and play. His dam had no scruples about snatching the most luscious patches from him so that he found it wiser to graze apart from her.

Little by little his independence grew. He still followed her when the herd was on the move, he still drew close to her at dusk to spend the night beside her, but during the day their paths hardly crossed for all that they were within calling distance.

The colt was gregarious by nature and had no desire to be alone. He struck up a friendship with another colt of about his own age, a bay with a twisted white blaze, and they were always together. They grazed side by side, their muzzles often touching as they searched after the same sweet grass, and when they were not grazing they would stand head to tail, swishing the flies from each other's unprotected flank. They fought mock battles, rearing, nipping, squealing, and they hardly noticed the existence of their earlier playmates, engrossed in each other's company.

II

The winter passed as uneventfully as the summer. Except that the grass shot up ever more abundantly so that the

horses grew fat and hardly moved, the foal discovered
that the weather was not so friendly as in the summer. It
gradually grew colder and colder and even though the
hair on his body grew thicker and fat began to form under
his skin there were many mornings that began in miserable
shiverings and nights when the frost was so thick that his
breath hung frozen on the air. The grass froze also and
lost its sweetness and the ground grew hard again, as in
summer.

Before the frost, there were many weeks of almost
incessant rain when the earth was covered with lakes and
churned with mud. Winter birds settled on the lakes and
were in their element while the horses stared miserably
at the flooded meadows and chewed at the soggy fodder
with little appetite. In the summer it was pleasant to be
covered with mud so that the flies could not bite but in
the winter the mud was clammy and never dried and the
horses were cold and uncomfortable. They had no protection against the downpours from the sky and stood with
drooping heads while the heavy rain bounced off their
backs and poured down their flanks. The sun had deserted
them and the sky was always white and grey-streaked
with clouds.

But even winter did not last for ever and gradually the
skies began to clear again, the sun to shine more linger-
ingly, the showers to become less frequent. The birds that
had fled the pampa during its coldness began to return
and the days were filled with the noise of them as in great
colonies they squabbled and searched for old nests or
fought over new ones. The sheets of rain-water shrank and
began to disappear and occasionally there were days
when the sun was really hot and vapour rose from the
earth to hang in clouds above the grass.

The horses began to cast their shaggy winter coats and most of them looked unkempt, dirty and ragged. The albino was no exception. He was almost a yearling now and no longer sucked his mother's milk. His fatness was a grass fatness and though there were strong muscles beneath his skin they hardly showed for the plumpness the heavy winter grazing had given him.

But with the change in the weather and the skylarks and lapwings soaring in the sky or drumming in the grass, the colts and fillies grew skittish again. The bright sun put spring in their hooves and, although all winter they had almost forgotten how to play, they suddenly remembered again and throughout the whole herd the youngsters began to frisk and gambol and toss their heads, throwing off the sluggishness of winter.

The albino and the bay with the crooked blaze took to racing each other across the flat grasslands. They raced with a grace that was beautiful to behold, as free as the swans that flew over their heads; their long legs outstretched, almost floating over the grass in their joy; their heads high, eyes brilliant with delight; tails and manes and forelocks combed out behind them by the wind. Sometimes the albino would draw ahead, sometimes the bay, and sometimes they would swirl in midflight to prance and rear and snort in pretended rage, feeling for the first time the stallion blood that was in them. They pawed at each other but with careful hooves. They circled and whickered and walked on their hindlegs. Then of one accord they would break into a gallop again and one would chase the other, snapping at the rump in front.

Such was the surging of springtime in their blood that they hardly thought of grazing nor even felt hunger. They

would snatch a few mouthfuls of grass or thistles then buck
and toss and swirl about; and sometimes the two of them
would pound wildly through the centre of a bunch of
staidly grazing matrons, or send a colony of peewits into
scandalous outcry with the impatience of their flying
hooves.

Mostly they raced, on and on and on, using up their
eternal energy, circling the herd at such a distance that
in the whole day they would hardly see a member of it.
They were always in each other's company and returned
only to their dams at nightfall, when their brazen courage
would desert them somewhat, frightened away by the
haunting cries of the crazy-widow birds or the scent of a
lion in the grass.

Then they would fall to grazing seriously, weary of
running and playing, ravenously hungry. The albino
would cling to his dam, a foal again, and rub himself
against her, seeking her caresses; and somewhere among
the shadows of dark bodies the bay would be doing the
same.

III

The vizcachas dug long, deep and complicated tunnels
beneath the pampa grass, throwing out the earth behind
them in huge mounds. Somewhere under these mounds,
in darkness and secrecy and freedom from danger, the
young of the vizcachas were born and nursed. The big
rheas made themselves an untidy nest in the middle of a
bunch of giant thistles, wild artichokes or plumy pampa
grass. They laid big eggs from which eventually hatched
the baby rheas, as wily from birth and as swift as their
parents. The skylarks nested in tussocks of grass; the wild
duck among the cane-brakes and amid the rushes along

the edges of a water course.

The deer and the guanaco dropped their young in a secluded place and within an hour the babies were running at their heels, the guanacos as white and woolly as the spring clouds. The rats, the armadillos, the snakes, each found a place in which to bring forth its young; even the fearsome lion nested somewhere on the pampa. And the horses were like the deer and the guanaco and the wild cattle they occasionally encountered. They drew away from the herd to a private place and returned only when the youngling could follow and more or less defend itself.

Thus it was that one day when the albino returned from his games and his races with the bay colt he looked in vain for his mother. He went from group to group in search of her, stopping to snatch a few mouthfuls of grass every now and then, not really perturbed for his need of her was automatic rather than essential. But as each mare turned her back on him or shouldered him away, not wanting him near her, a certain anxiety began to niggle at him, born of custom and a fear of loneliness.

His search grew more determined and he forgot the grass that had before distracted him. He came across the bay colt, grazing just a few yards from his dam. The albino whinnied and his companion looked up with pricked ears but was not tempted to follow him. Night was coming on. The individual outlines of the horses were fading into one long irregular shadow. Lions prowled in the grass at night and a colt was wise who stayed with his mother.

For a while the albino stopped beside the bay, grazing with him. But every few seconds he would raise his head and look about him anxiously and, seeing that his companion cared nothing for his plight, he eventually went away and continued his search.

For most of the night the albino colt looked for his mother and called in vain for her. He gained a few nips and kicks from the other mares, whom he startled in the darkness, but sympathy from none. Never had he noticed before how dark and how long was the night. He was afraid to lie down, having no mother to watch over him, and he was afraid to be alone. But there was no other mare that wanted him near and he wandered disconsolately from group to group, standing for a while at a short distance from them, trying to find comfort just in the presence of the other mothers, hoping perhaps that one of them would accept him.

Little by little his head drooped and his weary legs tired of constant movement. Each halt became more prolonged until in the end, overcome by misery and weariness, he found himself a spot alone from which he could at least see the rest of the herd and gain some comfort, and there with the moon glistening upon his white flanks, but with no mother to watch over him, he fell asleep.

The next day he played as usual with the bay colt and while he was racing and rearing and cavorting in the sunshine he forgot his loneliness and outcast state. It was only at dusk that he again remembered and for a second time began the fruitless search for the mother he had inexplicably lost. The second night he passed as he had done the first, lingering long in the company of the bay colt but unable to dispel the desolation that crept over him with the deepening of the darkness and the wild cries of the animals that lived on the fringes of the horse community.

The third night, too, was the same for him, looking for his dam and feeling fear and loneliness without her.

Now he was afraid to leave the herd, sensing somehow that she must return and wanting to be there waiting for her. He was impatient of the bay's efforts to draw him away and played only half-heartedly before breaking off and circling back to the herd. The colt followed, teasing and coaxing with many head tossings, pawings and whickerings, but the albino knew that his mother would come and spent best part of the morning pacing with that high, showy gait of his, back and forth, back and forth.

The bay colt tired and went away. Later he came back and still the albino kept the vigil for his mother. His companion joined him and for a while they cropped the grass, side by side, noses touching, and they lifted their heads simultaneously every now and then to watch the horizon, both beautiful in their alert youthfulness.

Suddenly the albino's instinct was rewarded. Before the afternoon was far advanced he saw his mother jogging towards him. At least he thought she was coming towards him but he noticed how she stopped every now and then to look back and seemed not to care at all that he was waiting for her. He called shrilly to her, filled with joy, but she made no answer and seemed to be unaware of his existence.

He threw himself at a gallop to meet her but drew to a halt before he was close enough to touch her. At her heels tottered a lank brown foal, walking stiff with uncertainty, and it was this odd creature that held all the mare's attention. The albino felt hostility in her as he approached and because of this he hesitated.

This was his mother and yet she was his dam no longer. This was what he smelt in her and it bewildered him exceedingly. The foal meant nothing to him. He could not connect it with his dam. He took no heed of his

mother's warning actions and drew close as always to be
caressed by her.

He was too close to avoid the teeth that suddenly tore
at him and drew back with a squeal of pain, a patch of
blood rapidly staining his pure white flank. This was no
admonishing nip that held a caress even while it punished
and the colt was halted in his tracks, utterly disconcerted.
Again his mother ignored him, interested only in the foal,
but when the albino warily tried to follow beside her also
she assaulted him a second time and drove him off with
whirlwind fury, teeth and hooves and squealing rage.

The albino fled, ears flattened and eyes wild with fear.
He had no memory of a time when he had come inno-
cently at the heels of his dam, like the brown foal now,
to dispossess a brother as now he was dispossessed.

For several days he hung about his mother, unable to
believe that not only did she no longer want him near
her but would actually attack him if he drew too close.
His cloud-white hide was bruised by her hooves and teeth
and he almost forgot the existence of the bay colt, engrossed by his dam's strange behaviour and the foal that
clung to her flank and eyed him with fear. But when at
last he realised that his mother would never revoke her
rejection of him he tired of hanging about her and once
again went in search of the other colt.

He found the bay deserted like himself, for his dam, too,
had another youngling tottering at her heels. They
rubbed noses and exchanged greetings then, of one
accord, broke into a wild, head-tossing gallop and fled
from the herd as if lions were after them. The thunder of
their hooves startled the placidly grazing mares and even
caused the stallion to lift his head and watch them for a
moment, wondering at their excitement.

4 : Pampa fire

Several years went by. The colts grew and became
stallions and still they followed the herd, part of it and
yet apart. Both developed into magnificent animals,
proud with youth and strength. Their long solid bodies
rippled with muscles and the sun on their backs made the

gloss of their coats seem even brighter. The albino
especially was beautiful with a heavy mane that cascaded
to his withers, a thick forelock that almost hid his eyes and
a banner-like tail that swept through the grasses.

The two animals played less often now, though they
continued to graze amicably in each other's company,
nose to tail, swishing the flies from each other's flanks and
withers. When they played their mock battles were
inclined to become real ones for neither was as placid as
their still figures would suggest. An accidental blow with
a hoof would cause the stallion tempers to boil. The
pricked ears would flatten, teeth were bared, and a clash
was inevitable if one or the other was disinclined to
submit.

With the leader of the herd they were afraid to battle.
The old, one-eyed stallion still held full sway over his
mares and any of his sons that tried to steal them from
him soon regretted it. He was implacable in his rage. No
one blow or two would satisfy him. He would chase his
usurpers across the pampa for miles, forcing them into
self-defence and battering them with his hard, experienced
hooves and teeth until they bowed their heads in total
submission.

Both the bay and the albino, young stallions still,
respected him too much to try to steal his mares. They
would haze around them when they could, exchange a few
grunts and caresses, but the mares grew noisy and excited
in the presence of another stallion so that soon the old
one would grow aware of the situation and be down upon
the thieves with a squeal of fury in his tnroat that was
usually enough to frighten them away. His sons would
retire to a safe distance, watching the mares and impatiently stamping, sometimes shaking their heads in anger

at the old stallion but not daring to accept his challenge or to go closer while he watched them.

Neither ever thought of leaving the herd and going his own way in search of mares for himself. The pampa was wide and lonely for a solitary animal, with not even a tree to shade him from the sun and perhaps a lion lurking behind every tuft of grass. The sight, smell or even sound of the big herd was a necessary comfort to the two animals that grazed otherwise alone. They had been born within its radius and it was as much a part of their existence as the sky and the earth and the revolving seasons.

II

It was during the albino stallion's sixth summer that the first real danger came to threaten him and it came in an insidious fashion, a scent in the breeze that caused him to wrinkle his pink nostrils for a moment and raise his head as he sought to recognise it. Then the breath of danger disappeared before the albino could puzzle over it and he began to graze again, the thing forgotten.

The sun was hot that day, perhaps the hottest of all that long and weary summer, and it was only the changeable breeze that made it bearable. The two stallions sought spasmodically among the withered grass and flowers for something worth eating and now and again one or the other would lift his head and widen his nostrils, scenting again the puzzling odour that came with the wind. By nightfall the heat had not abated and all the horses of the herd were restless. The strange scent was stronger now and because they could not recognise it they were disturbed.

The old stallion wheeled constantly about his herd,

grunting and whistling through his nostrils, pushing the straggling mares into some semblance of solidity. Fear was growing within him, perhaps instinctive, perhaps remembered, and this it was that made him bunch his big herd together, mares and fillies and the foals that followed them. He snapped and struck at the yearling colts that attempted to cling too closely to the herd. They were no longer his responsibility, his future enemies in fact, and in times of threatened danger tolerance was forgotten.

But the night passed uneventfully, a clear half moon casting gloomy light over the dry grasslands and nervous horses. The breeze continued to carry the insidious warning, recognised by the horses but not understood.

The sun came to the sky in a mist of orange light and as the morning progressed the sky grew yellow instead of blue. Now was the scent much stronger on the breeze that bowled playfully towards the herd and a noise was growing among its members as mares whickered nervously or whinnied to their younglings.

The breeze was heavy with the acrid smell of burnt cane, thistle and dried grass and, as the day progressed and the sky loured over them, there was no freshness left in it at all. Its gusts came thick with smoke and the horizon was blurred as if with fog.

Slowly, still not fully aware of the danger that threatened them, the herd began to move with the breeze and the satellite animals like the albino and the bay followed. The sky grew darker, the horses began to snort and neigh as the clean air was swallowed up relentlessly minute by minute. A flock of rheas came running alongside the horses, covering the pampa in huge, effortless strides. Soon the rheas were far ahead, a straggling herd of guanacos behind them, and the horses caught their alarm and began to move faster.

But a jogging, bewildered mass of animals cannot move as swiftly as an unfettered wind and soon the horizon was broken with streaks of light amidst the greyness, flickering low at first, then shooting into lively, dancing sheets of brightness. The pampa was on fire.

How quickly did those giddy tongues of fire travel, borne by the breeze that knew no halting. For three days it had burned already and its rapacious hunger was increased by what it fed on, a thirsty pampa thick with dry thistle and bracken, carpeted with wilted grass and flowers. The vizcachas and the armadillos were suffocated in their holes, the ground birds roasted in their nests, and the rheas, the guanacos, the horses fled until their eyes bulged and their hearts burst and the flames overtook them.

The fire was as fickle as the breeze that bore it, turning first this way and then another, devouring creatures that had the day before escaped and now lay panting and at rest, believing themselves to be free of danger.

The scorching heat reached the horses long before the flames and those that came behind grew wild with fear and pushed against the rumps in front of them, fighting for a passageway through them. The jogging gait had grown into a canter, the canter to a gallop and even as the horizon burst into flame the whole herd of some eight hundred animals was thundering across the still free grassland ahead of them, necks stretched out, tails streaming.

They ran blindly, fear their master, and there was no mare mother enough to desert the dash for safety to heed a youngling left behind, bawling terror, and desolation. The herd streamed out into a long, thick line, the swift to the fore, the old, the lame, the weary bringing up the tail-end. The one-eyed stallion led them but ahead of him, though at a wide distance, raced his two throw-back sons, the albino and the bay.

Birds flew up under the stampeding hooves to be crushed and left to the flames that followed. A herd of deer bounded alongside the horses and for once the latter were unaware of them. There were only two smells on the pampa now, one of fear, the other of fire.

All day the fire followed the herd, sometimes rapidly, little tongues of flame licking over the dry grass in streams, to be followed by the cascade of smoke and fire in its wake. Other times it was held back by the changing wind, seemingly straining against the force that tethered it and searching to east and west for outlet. Lone animals were left behind in the smoke, exhausted or lamed, shadows until the fire took them. And the big herd of eight hundred had become scattered bunches of still fleeing horses, no longer united, each one living in his own world of terror and oblivious of the rest.

The old stallion still kept well to the fore, as well as most of the younger animals, but of them all the albino and his companion were at the best advantage for they had left the herd behind long since, from the beginning unhampered. These two raced side by side as often they had raced in fun, only now their eyes bulged with strain, their mouths sawed at the dry air, breath rasped in their throats and their glossy coats were dirty with sweat and the dust of the fire which coated them with greyness.

By nightfall they had gained enough on their relentless pursuer to pause for rest. But it was an alert, uneasy rest and they thought not of grazing nor felt hunger. Both

were desperately thirsty, for the air was dry with the heat
of the fire and thick with ash which floated in the breeze,
but in this part there was no water. Even the breeze
was hot and tickled their wide-stretched nostrils, offering
them no alleviation, and the two young stallions did not
rest for long. Terror was still their companion and long
before the darkness of the night was broken they were off
at a canter again, and the sound of their hooves was loud
over the unusually silent pampa.

Southwards they travelled and some two hours after
they had left their resting place the flames had reached
it. They did not halt as had done the stallions but continued their swirling, devouring dance, and the night
sky glowed redly as it reflected the fire that refused to die.
Between the two stallions and the fire was only the empty
pampa. The rest of the herd was somewhere lost, over-
taken by the flames perhaps, and even its wily, one-eyed
leader did not come prancing and blowing nor would do
so again.

On and on the two stallions fled and the bay's eyes grew
as red as the albino's. Now and again they mingled with
rheas and guanacos or with other horses but they shied
from numbers and ran faster alone. They came eventually
to a river, wide and slow and marshly, its level much sunk
because of the summer heat which had sucked its moisture,
and into this they gratefully plunged.

The water caressed their exhausted bodies and they
stood up to their bellies in it for an hour or more, drinking
avidly until their thirsts were satiated. Then, more slowly,
they struggled through its depths and came to shore on a
muddy bank where ducks sunned themselves and a few
herons dozed on one leg, seemingly unaware of the fire
that raged at so little distance from them.

The horses were affected by the tranquillity of the place and they made another halt, snatching at the grass that still grew greenly along the bank. The fire reached the horizon and the stallions snorted, shook their heads and trembled. They wheeled away from the river and startled the ducks with the terror-struck sound of their hooves.

The fire reached the river and there at last it was halted for the breeze was tired of playing with the flames and deserted them on the bank instead of blowing them across. The river was too wide to be leapt by even the most avid of fires and for several hours it swept up and down the long, long bank of the river, searching, devouring, tiring, dying.

The water birds had fled to its other bank and, crouched among the cool rushes, watched the monster gradually die, leaving a scorched, blackened shadow of itself over all the pampa. For days afterwards smoke rose up from the earth, thin and grey, and the ducks could not return to their side of the river without burning themselves.

Miles to the south the two stallions had halted. The breeze was no longer heavy with burning and instead blew sweetly fresh from the colder, southern lands. They came back to the river in search of water and fresh grazing, but they could not return to their old grazing grounds for there was nothing left but the smell of terror and the smoke that continued to spiral upwards.

5 : Gauchos

The pampa that had always seemed so free from danger now began to show its other nature to the two stallions, first in the all-destructive fire of which they were reminded for a long time because of the acrid smell which was blown to them whenever the wind came from across the burnt-

out grasslands, and then in another more violent manner
when for the first time in their six summers of life they
were pursued and captured by the only creature on the
pampa they knew not of, man.

They had grazed beside the rheas and the guanacos all
their lives; they had slept at night with the voices of the
vizcachas booming in their ears and the scratchings and
whisperings of other rodents a comforting accompaniment;
they knew all the birds, both large and small, and they
had even gone stiff with fright sometimes at the rank smell
of lion which lingered in some brackeny spot where a
puma had nested. But of this other creature that rode
upon the backs of their own kind and made slaves of
them, and was greater in wile, persistence and cruelty
than all of their few enemies, they knew nothing.

Their first awareness of man's existence came one
early morning when they were grazing beside that same
river which had previously saved their lives. The sky was
still dark in the west and the moon hanging palely there.
Over the water hung a lacy mist which clung to the webs
spun by spiders among the rushes. It was a time of silence
on the pampa, when the night animals had returned to
their underground holes, the nightbirds to their nests,
and the day creatures had not yet ventured from sleeping.

The two stallions stood at the water's edge, quenching
their thirsts unhurriedly, and the albino was hardly more
than a shadow in the milk-coloured mist. He lifted his
head, ears pricked, having caught the faintest of sounds
in those silent moments. The bay was soon in following
his example and the two stood alert and listening for
the sound was that of their own kind, that of galloping
hooves. The sound came from the other side of the river,
across the fire-scorched earth, and the stallions quivered

with anticipation as they listened. Since the fire they had neither seen nor heard any of their own kind.

As they listened and waited the sun broke through the mist. Darkness fled, though the moon lingered some minutes longer, and the stallions caught sight of those travelling so swiftly towards them.

It was a troup of some three dozen horses and the stallions watched with interest, sensing no danger, though the galloping hooves filled them with restlessness and set their own hooves dancing over the soft soil beside the river. They wheeled about, whickered and snorted, and even though they eventually became aware of the strange, almost bird-like creatures the two leading horses carried on their backs, in their innocence they were unafraid.

And so they waited, until the gauchos were close enough to frighten them with their loud shrieks, their cracking whips, the roughness of their movements, the total strangeness of their appearance and smell. Then the two stallions fled. The calm of the morning was broken by loud turbulent splashes as the gauchos forded the river in pursuit of the two beautiful animals they had unexpectedly roused, and by their triumphant shouts of laughter as they urged on their mounts and whirled the bolas about their heads.

The bay let out a squeal as he crashed to the ground and a second later the albino was flung to the earth also, his hindlegs entangled by the stones and leather which had wound themselves about him in half a dozen twirls. He screamed with surprise and fear, lashed out with all four legs and rolled and twisted on the ground. But the thongs only tightened themselves about him, increasing his fear and rage.

He made several vain efforts to rise to all fours and for

a moment stood clumsily before plunging himself off balance again, and then the horses and their gaucho riders were upon him and he became their captive.

A lasso was put round his neck in spite of his plunging hooves and head. With the same length of cord they tied up his off foreleg and pulled up the knee to the level of his chin so that although he could stand he could not move, as he learnt after several clumsy falls. Thus they left him while they went to remove the bolas from the bay and halter him in a similar fashion.

Then they went back across the river to hobble their bell-mares and assure that their horses did not stray. They were deaf to the distressed cries of the two captive stallions, plunging and falling and vainly fighting the cords that held them, and were as thrilled as children with a new toy, exclaiming over the beauty of the two animals and of the fun they would have trying to ride them.

The sky was blue now and the moon had vanished. The mist no longer hung over the river nor clung to the cobwebs in the rushes, but the water birds did not come out of their sleeping places, frightened by the cries and snorts of the two stallions and the sound of the men who had come to disturb the tranquillity of the pampa.

II

On those wide and empty grasslands which were still half unexplored and whose soil was still almost completely unbroken by the tools of man, compassion, gentleness and understanding were unknown qualities. The horses knew nothing of them and neither did the men. They were two brute forces, competing one against the other. The horses had the greater strength, the men the greater cunning and cruelty. The horses expected to suffer at the hands of their captors, for this they feared them so greatly, and the men would inflict suffering upon them for it was the only kind of strength they knew. They laughed and joked with each other as the stallions trembled and the birds stayed hidden in the rushes, and they advanced upon their captives.

Tethering their own mounts to a tussock of grass, with the swiftness of the slow-moving armadillo when it digs itself a hole they released the two stallions from their crippling postures and were upon their backs. The reaction of the bay and the albino was simultaneous. Both squealed with fear and rage and reared, their front legs savagely pawing the air. The gauchos yelled and beat at them with their whips and the horses forgot the existence of each other, engrossed in their own private world of battle.

The cries of the men and horses mingled and echoed across the pampa and dust flew up from the dry ground, smarting in their eyes. The albino twisted and reared and bucked and tried in every possible way to remove the creature that clung to his back, raking him with huge, three-pointed spurs, thrashing his head and rump with the whip; and the bay did likewise. At times they were close together, but not seeing each other; at times they were far apart, and the two horses that watched them rolled their eyes and tugged against the reins that restrained them, sharing the fear of their wild brothers, perhaps remembering their own initiation into the ways of the gauchos.

Never had the albino felt such hot anger and terror, and the two combined made him ignore all weariness and pain. Though his heart pounded with giddying force, though his legs trembled and threatened to forsake him, though his mouth and nostrils were choked with dust and froth and his flanks were raw and bloody where the spurs punished him, he would recognise no end to the battle until the monstrous thing that clung to him was beneath his hooves and vanquished.

Squeals of anger became squeals of desperation and when he could no longer voice his terror loudly he grunted and snorted and tossed even more wildly. But the man on his back was impervious to all his raging and as tireless as he was exhausted. There seemed to be no way of dislodging him until suddenly the bay stallion collapsed. For no more than half a second was the attention of the albino's rider diverted but it was all that the desperate horse was looking for.

He nearly dislocated his back with the last desperate lunge that he gave, his legs stiff, his chin almost touching his belly, and a wild cry of triumph escaped him as he felt the gaucho slipping. One more toss and he was free. The gaucho was stumbling on the ground beside him and, before he could regain his balance and grab the halter, the albino was away, racing as he had never raced in all his life.

Free of the gaucho, his frenzy subsided and his long legs swept over the dry pampa with the ease of a bird caught in the wind. He galloped with his head held high and proudly, and when he finally halted he was a long way from the scene of the battle and his whole body trembled with weariness. Now did he begin to feel the stinging cuts slashed in his flanks by the spurs, now did he realise that the halter was still about his head, its rope trailing along the ground. Now also did he realise that he was alone. For the first time the bay stallion had not followed him.

For all his weariness the albino could not rest. He kept circling about, uttering short whinnies and grunts, pawing at the ground. Now and again he shook his head impatiently or tried to rub off the halter against a front leg and often he looked in the direcion from which he had come, scenting the river water in the wind and the faint smell of burning which still hung over the pampa. But the bay stallion did not come, nor even the scent of him, and the albino whickered softly to himself, disconsolate.

He grazed for a while, snatching at a few unpalatable patches of grass, and then the sharp cry of a bird startled him and he set off at a gallop again as if pursued. The rope jerking along beside him added to his terror and he fled from it in vain.

For best part of the day he kept on running, frightened by the slightest sound or movement, but when night came and with it the usual nocturnal sounds and activities, his fear faded. He had learned to interpret the sounds of the rodents and knew by listening to them that they were tranquil, and so at last he stopped running away.

The moon illuminated his solitary whiteness on the lonely plain as he stood with drooping body in a dozing state. Now and again he roused himself to rub again at the halter and, with wakefulness, he would realise that he was alone. Three times in the night he called to the bay with loud, echoing neighs that startled the vizcachas, and the only answer that came back to him was the unchanging sounds of the pampa night.

The gauchos had taken his companion as they would have taken him and for a while the albino felt as lonely as a motherless foal for never had he grazed without the bay somewhere near. He would look up from eating with pricked ears, wondering for a moment where the other was, and then he would remember. And when he cantered or galloped the sound of his hooves was a lonely one, for it was no longer echoed by those of the bay.

Hatred grew in the heart of the albino, the first he had ever experienced, and it was a hatred particularly intense for at the same time he was afraid. The bay had been his shadow for a lifetime and now all that he had was the memory of the gauchos' violence and their rope about his head.

6 : Terror

All that summer and the following winter the white stallion dwelt alone and his solitary state lay heavily upon him. He had never lived without the sound and smell of the herd, nor without the presence of the bay, and his unanswered neighs and whinnies filled him with a sense of loneliness. He managed to rid himself of the rope that had molested him; his scarred flanks healed and were hidden by the hair that grew thickly over them; the memory of that violent morning faded, but his loneliness grew greater.

At the coming of spring, when the peewits and plover were preening themselves and courting and all the birds were busy with nest-making, when the larks flooded the early mornings with music and the fleecy young of the guanacos were gambolling in the new grass, the albino knew that he could dwell alone no longer. Instinct impelled him to search out his own kind and for many days he wandered, tearing at the new grass as he went, smelling and listening and calling.

He was beautiful in his eagerness, his white head proudly held, his high, free gait a princely movement, his coat as pure as swan's down. As free as the birds that nested at his hooves, the pampa he trod over was his own, and the blood thrilled within him at the pure joy of being alive with the wind in his nostrils and the sun on his back and the never-ending plains to race over.

He raced with the joy of a bird in flight and at times was hardly more than a colt in his enthusiasm, bucking, snorting, pretending fear at his own shadow or the rustle of the wind through the thistles. But when at last there was the smell of horses in the air, the scent of other stallions, his playfulness fell away.

Arrogance overcame prudence. He swept about the herd with an airy gallop, calling to the mares, challenging the colts and stallions, and all was confusion among them at the sight and sound of this haughty, fearless intruder.

Tranquillity was lost among the excited whickerings of the mares that answered him, the colts that felt his challenge but shrank from answering it. Only one voice echoed in answer to the albino's own, that of the small herd's master, and he came out from among the mass of horses, slowly but unafraid, walking on his hindlegs and pounding the ground with his front hooves, his throat full of angry whistlings.

He was a strong, good-looking stallion, hardly any older than the albino, mealy-coloured, his vision half lost behind an unchecked forelock, his small ears already champed in another battle. The albino ignored him and swept once more about the herd as if to show the other that from this day onwards it would be his, and its master squealed a second warning, flinging into it a righteous challenge.

The albino checked his course. The smell of the herd excited him and filled his whole being with the determination to possess it, and now he advanced upon the black-maned lord that crashed angry hooves to the ground, whistling his own imperious anger.

The mares drew back in timid fear as the two male animals suddenly engaged in combat. The albino attacked with the fury of the usurper determined to win, the other defending his right with equal rage. There was the sound of hooves striking on flesh, of teeth that clashed as they sought for each other's throats, and not for a moment did they stand off and rest for both were young and rage-filled and the heat of their blood made them heedless of wounds. There was no bluff, no caution, no quarter yielded. They tore at each other with all their savage stallion anger until one would give way or be crushed.

The mealy-coloured stallion was smaller than his adversary and eventually the difference began to tell. Both were torn and bloody in many places but it was not until the albino brought down a hoof that landed sharply on the other's skull that the battle ended. The smaller horse staggered under the blow and his legs doubled under him. The albino renewed his attack as the other quavered and might have killed him had not the other found the last-minute strength that kept him from sprawling. Instead he dragged himself away from the albino's reach and all his proud anger was gone. His blood-matted head drooped and the white stallion knew that he was vanquished.

He advanced threateningly and the other backed a few paces more, offering no defence except in admitting his defeat. With this the albino was satisfied but he continued to chivvy his adversary until at last this latter was at a good distance from the herd that had been his, outcast from it for ever.

The albino returned to his newly won mares which had gone back to grazing, uninterested in the fate of their former lord, and in turn they crowded about him. There was much whickering and squealing as they smelled at him and accepted him and in these first moments of possession and glory the white stallion took no heed of the gashes in his neck and withers and flanks, cleft by the other's hooves and round which the flies were already buzzing. He accepted the mares' caresses, offered some of his own, and when this was done he sought out the colts and gave them a taste of his heels and teeth so that they should learn to respect him.

In the afternoon he fought two minor battles with a couple of younger stallions that had for the past year been kept in check by the strength of the other, and both he cast out from the herd, permitting them no quarter for they would be his enemies always.

By nightfall he was overcome with weariness and his wounds were beginning to ache, but he moved among his newly acquired mares proud and contented, sniffing at one, nipping another, while in the distance the young outcast stallions watched him rancorously. The albino was aware of them but untroubled. For the moment at least he was king.

II

More than a year went by and the albino stallion lived in tranquillity with his mares. The herd numbered just over a hundred, including the young colts and the foals, and it was a small one in comparison with the one that the albino had previously known. However he was well content for all of them were his and he had no memory now of that other herd with its fearful one-eyed stallion. Neither did he remember the bay colt nor even the fire. The only thing that stayed in his memory was his fear of man and this remained because more than once in that year did he see an occasional horse and rider.

The slightest glimpse was all he needed to feel again the rage and desperation that had filled him and it was almost as if he could still feel the gaucho on his back and his shouts in his ears. He would prance and snort with shaking head, then gather up his mares and lead them to what he considered to be a safer place.

What the stallion did not know was that there were various small ranches on that side of the river and even a hamlet beyond the horizon. Cattle and sheep grazed over that part of the pampa and when the stallion sometimes spied them from a distance he would draw hurriedly away, for with them came the smell of man. He kept the mares almost endlessly on the move until he was satisfied that there was no danger.

But the albino had no knowledge of the ways of man, only of other animals like himself that would not molest him if he left them alone. His instinct told him that if he moved away they would not touch him and so he kept on moving, erratically southwards, feeling in this way safe. He could not know that men might covet him for his beauty, or his mares for their skins and their heavy tails, and that leaving him in peace now was not a promise that they never would molest him.

So it was that on a warm morning half way between spring and summer, when the albino felt himself safe and the memory of man had almost faded, he heard again the wild shrieks that had set his blood pounding and saw in the distance a number of gauchos travelling towards him. His reaction was as it had been that other time. He fled, giving no thought to the mares that were his pride, and they seeing his fear and hearing the far-off noises grew agitated and fearful also.

Within minutes all were copying his example and the tranquil day thundered with the sound of their hooves. Birds flew up in fright and flapped over the backs of the stampeding horses; a herd of deer caught the fear and with grass still between their jaws leaped alongside them.

They fled towards the unhampered east but suddenly there were gauchos in that direction too, and the stallion, seeing them first, reared and swerved towards the south. But here were still more men and horses and these were followed by dogs that loudly yammered their blood-lust, and for all that the albino changed direction, racing hither and thither, wherever he went he encountered more gauchos.

The mares, confused and terrified, scattered in every direction. They collided into each other, dashing about like ants on an upset ant-hill, and around them galloped the stallion, neighing shrilly, as terrified and as confused as they.

The gauchos closed in on them and the sound of the bolas swirling above their heads was like the rushing of a winter wind. The deadly weapons left their owners' hands and within seconds horses were beginning to stagger and fall. Once they were down there was no getting up, for even as they struggled to all fours the gaucho to whom the bolas belonged would be upon his prey. One spring from the saddle, one slash with his knife, and the horse would be either hamstrung or pulsing out its life from a severed jugular, and then the gaucho was up again, the bolas swinging once more, to chase after another vainly fleeing mare.

There were some thirty men and a hundred horses and the hunt lasted over a distance of four or five miles, miles that became littered with gasping, fallen bodies as one by one the free ones were pulled down. And when there remained but three or four horses the gauchos suddenly became aware of the stallion that led them, racing like a cloud with the wind behind it, beautiful in his wild frenzy.

'For me!' cried one, standing up in the stirrups to broadcast his claim.

'For me!' cried the rest almost simultaneously, and the dead and dying horses they had left behind them were suddenly forgotten as they set out upon this new chase, each one intent to have the fabulous stallion for himself.

But their mounts were already tired and beginning to flag in spite of the excited spurs that tore at them mercilessly, and the albino had never galloped so swiftly nor been so afraid. He left the few remaining mares behind as, with eyes bulging and heart almost bursting, he flung himself headlong in the only direction left open to him and which would lead to freedom if only he could outpace the terrible hunters who came on behind.

It seemed that he would never rid himself of their savage whoopings but bit by bit his superior stature and strength began to tell and the gauchos grew more furious in their spurrings as they realised that the stallion was outpacing them. Several began whirling their bolas to throw after him in a vain attempt to check his flight but the distance was too great and the bolas swung helplessly, winding themselves about the grass tussocks when thrown but missing the white stallion's fetlocks.

Then the gauchos remembered that they had work to do on the plain behind them and regretfully they checked their mounts and turned them back to the scene of the hunt. The dying horses must be finished off and all had to be skinned. They jogged back to their work cursing the stallion that had escaped them but at the same time admiring his beauty, his speed, his grace, his wildness . . . Everything about him. And each man in his heart determined upon the albino for himself while saying nothing to his fellows.

III

When the gauchos had gone from that part of the pampa the albino returned. More than a week had passed by but still the fear had not left him. There was hardly any place where he could sojourn without seeing or hearing them for they were hunting over the whole district for the hides of horses or wild cattle and the feathers of the rheas. For the whole week the albino had kept on running, first to the west, then to the north, eastwards, southwards, wherever he could to escape the gauchos.

Had he forgotten the terrible extermination of his herd he would have been soon reminded by the smell of rotting carcasses that clung to the air in that part and the sight of the heavy-bellied hawks that could not even move in their fullness.

Terror and disgust were mingled as he wheeled about the place and once again he fled, hardly knowing where he could go to escape the slaughterers that had suddenly descended upon the tranquil pampa.

His wild eyes wide with panic, his sleek coat dank with sweat, his jaws half-open the better to suffer his thirst-swollen tongue, he galloped haphazardly from place to place, driven by fear and afraid to linger for more than a moment in any one spot. And without the hundred mares that had been his, whose carcasses were but meat for the scavengers, even loneliness terrified him.

7 : The lonely beach

Once the gauchos had seen the albino stallion and found
him so beautiful he knew no peace. There were men who
had wanted to forsake the hunt that very day in order to
chase after him and would have done so but that the one
in charge forbade them.

'There's time enough for chasing after fancies when the work is finished,' he told them. 'When this is done and you've all been paid then you can chase after a dozen white stallions if you wish.'

There were arguments among them, too, as to whom the stallion belonged, for most of them coveted him.

'He's mine. I saw him first,' said one.

'But if I catch him first I shall keep him,' another replied, and they squabbled and might even have ended the argument with their knives had not the one who led them been forceful in character and respected by all.

As it was they held themselves in check until their ox-waggons were creaking under the weight of skins and feathers which must be taken to the town; they waited until the money was shared out between them; they passed a few weeks spending it here and there, then those who were still interested returned to the place where they had first seen the stallion and set out in search of him.

By this time their imaginations had increased the stallion's propensities a hundred-fold. He was bigger than any animal they had ever seen and far more beautiful, swifter than the rushing winter winds and wilder, and they repeated the story so many times that eventually they came to believe it. They convinced themselves and their listeners that the stallion was a horse like no other.

Thus, as spring mellowed into summer, any number of gauchos set out in search of him. Some rode in twos or threes, some rode singly. Some tired of searching for him and were diverted to other things, but others were steadfast and spent the whole summer crossing and recrossing the district where first they had seen him and eventually he was discovered.

There was no mistaking him for another. His pure colouring, his stance, the magnificence of his features were enough to tell any gaucho—even those who had come in search of him on hearsay only—that this was the stallion they sought. But they soon discovered that it would not be easy to catch him.

The albino stallion had become the wariest of creatures now, shunning all company, made fearful by the first hoofbeat that reached his hearing. When the sound of a galloping horse came to his ears long before it was within his sight he would be away, his ears flattened, his tail held high and streaming out behind him, and rarely did the gauchos see more than this, a fast-fleeing cloudlike creature already far beyond their reach.

They chased him into the darkness of the nights and in the mornings they set out in pursuit of him again, but with a man behind him the stallion never faltered and while the gauchos slept he would still keep running. In the darkest hours before dawn broke he would pause a while to draw in deep breaths of air and snatch at the thistles, and then he would be away again, fear stronger than weariness or hunger.

Although the gauchos' horses were then fresher than he, the men lost time searching for his tracks and it might take them half a day to find him, while in fast pursuit the stallion had the advantage, for he was swifter than the average pony, his legs much longer, and he carried no weight upon his back.

The summer days lost their freshness and became sullenly hot. Dark clouds gathered at times but a breeze would come up and push them away. The grass withered and the ground grew hard. The stallion was weary now and his pursuers were losing interest. Their first enthusiasm had died long since and only determination had kept them to the chase. But with the burning sun reflecting its heat both from the sky and the ground even determination wavered and it was difficult to find the albino's tracks on the hard baked earth.

There came a day when the stallion instinctively knew that no one was following him. He was still cautious, he still kept moving, but the whole day passed without sighting a single gaucho. That night he rested and tore at the faded grass with unsatisfied hunger. The next day he was off again but he was even more certain that no one pursued him. For two or three days more he kept up his flight but it was half-hearted now and he stopped occasionally to graze. Only when he was finally satisfied that his enemy had left him in peace did he relax.

He grazed and dozed and grazed some more but always his ears were alert for the slightest unusual sound. A startled bird was all he needed to set him off at a gallop. But the days passed by and nothing happened to disturb his tranquillity. He was thin and jaded and his proud head drooped but the victory was his and his spirit was as wild as ever.

II

Just because the gauchos had been unable to capture the stallion they could not forget him. All through the hot summer when they left him alone and spent their spare hours exchanging news at the nearest store, or when they lazed in the shadow of a solitary ombu tree sipping at the maté pot with friends and circulating stories, the elusive albino was mentioned and he became renowned for his speed and beauty.

Their imagination ever dwelling in the infinite world of

spirits and goblins, it did not take the gauchos long to decide that the animal was possessed, that perhaps in fact he did not exist at all but was a demon, appearing only to torment them and lead them to their doom should they insist upon following him. To what strange world would he take them, assuming that he was never lost from sight? Could any gaucho possibly ride him and what would become of the bold one that tried?

Such were the idle suppositions of the gauchos who were haunted by their own loneliness and populated it with unearthly beings. But even as they wondered thus it still occurred to them that he might just be a horse of flesh and blood, wilier, fleeter, more 'gaucho' than their own, and they spoke of taking up the chase again when the cooler weather returned.

So it was that as the summer birds began to grow restless, remembering the warmer northern lands, and the rivers and lakes were no longer graced with glowing flamingo colours, the gauchos were once again foraging the pampa for the albino stallion. Winter had come before they found him, for he had wandered a long way southwards, almost afraid of the green lands from which sprung so cruel and persistent an enemy. He had gone on and on until the winds that tickled his nostrils brought only the scent of ice and barrenness. Then he halted. The cold was piercing and he was not prepared for it.

He found himself among rocks and hard soil and stunted trees, where grass was difficult to discover and unsucculent, but at least he found peace there, which was all he sought. His hair grew thicker as the weather worsened and he accustomed himself to the land; to winds that howled and were ever constant; to the nighttime silence, for here the ground was too hard for the vizcachas to burrow. And although sometimes he would lift his head to breathe in the winds that had crossed the pampa, bringing with them a reminder of sweet alfalfa and other herbs, he stayed in this new place for there were no men there to molest him.

The days were often grey and as winter deepened an insidious mist crept over everything, giving strange un-earthly forms to the rocks and bushes. The stallion was disturbed at first by this strange element that clung so damply to him and through which he could hardly see at times. The mist had a salty taste for it came in from the great Atlantic which was not very far away and it left a tangy flavour on the grass and bushes. There were days when the darkness hardly lifted from the land; other days when it rained almost constantly; and although the stallion was unused to so harsh a climate he endured it because of the sanctuary it offered him.

But even there he discovered that his tranquillity was not to last, for again one day he heard the shouts of men and the wild galloping of their horses' hooves, and now he was truly desperate in his fear for it seemed that never would he be able to escape them. His lonely sojourn had not caused him to forget their callous ways and their brutality, and again he fled, not knowing where he could go in order to be rid of them for ever.

The chase this time was a sporadic one for the gloomy climate protected the stallion in its way, gathering him up in the mist which was as white as he and hiding him even from the gauchos' piercing eyes. Seeing him disap-pear with such rapidity they were even more convinced that the horse they sought to capture was but a spirit, for they also were unaccustomed to the sea mists that descended and lifted so rapidly.

'This is a terrain fit for devils,' said one when they had pulled up their mounts in confusion, hardly able to see more than a pace or two on either side. 'No wonder we should find him here.'

'Devil or not,' replied another, 'my Three Marias will take care of him.'

The 'Three Marias' referred to the three stone balls of the bolas, but before they could trip the stallion up they had to be within reach of him and in the sudden fogs it was difficult to find him. At times the albino would be hardly more than a mile ahead, stumbling over boulders, almost unable to run, and then when they thought he was theirs a blanket of white mist crossed their paths and the stallion had disappeared into it.

'It's a devil sent to torment us,' insisted the first gaucho again. 'I've never chased after any animal so long and still not been able to catch him. He'll lead us to damnation if we insist on following,' and he was all for turning back to a more Christian land where at least a man could see where he was going.

The others had more courage than their companion and were not afraid of challenging the devil for once in a while.

'Let's catch him and give him a good thrashing for our pains,' they said. 'We'll teach him not to be a devil.'

But the days passed when sometimes they saw him and sometimes they only heard him. He was never far beyond their reach for even the stallion could not travel very quickly. He rarely broke from a canter or a hurried trot for the land was rocky and loose with scree, and the mist that hid him from his pursuers also prevented him from making much progress. It seemed to the gauchos that he tormented them on purpose, always within their reach but so elusive. They cursed him and prayed to all the saints for assistance in the capture of him.

The face of the land changed again. Rocky ground gave way to sand. The few bushes and trees were all bent in a westerly direction, deformed by the constant wind, and the hills were hills of sand, dunes that constantly altered in height or thickness or position, according to the wind. Desperate was the horse that trod this forsaken countryside where not even a blade of grass would grow or a bird linger. Brave were the men who followed him who had never seen such countryside in all their lives and were already convinced that they were pursuing the very devil to his inferno.

Now the wind blew with vengeance, whipping the breath from the stallion's open jaws, almost choking him with its force. His red eyes stung with the salt that clung to the air, his tongue was swollen with thirst. There was a crashing sound in his ears, slow, persistent, eternal, a sound he had never heard before. But on he raced, not caring now where he went for still the gauchos were behind him and he knew that his energy was failing fast.

That day a strong wind blew in from the ocean. The mist lifted and the noise that had bewildered the stallion revealed itself as the motion of the sea, huge, grey waves that crashed upon the sand. Now the horse saw that he could go no farther. Ahead of him was the sea, cold, relentless. Behind him were the men.

He halted for a moment, his proud head lifted. The wind caught at the thick forelock and mane, blowing them back from his head and neck. His jaws were wide open, as were his nostrils, as vainly he tried to drag fresh energy into his burning lungs. His eyes seemed to glow in his desperation.

It was thus that the gauchos suddenly saw him and they pulled up their horses, hardly able to believe in what they saw. Surely there was no horse anywhere as beautiful as this one, that looked almost ready to spring up into the clouds in his effort to escape? Could it be an animal of flesh and blood, so white against the leaden sea, its eyes burning like two fires, its locks like the wings of the angels?

For several moments they hesitated, almost afraid to pursue him further, and even as they wondered and admired and doubted, the stallion saw them and knew that he was lost. He gave a wild and desperate neigh, which rang even above the sound of the crashing waves, and he paced along the beach with tossing head, beautiful in his terror.

The gauchos forgot their wonder. They split into two groups, hurriedly making plans. One group galloped to the north, another to the south, and on that long and lonely beach the stallion was trapped between them. From both directions they came rushing towards him, the sound of their horses thundering over the hard sand which was flung up on every side of them.

Still the stallion lingered, prancing in small circles, his beautiful head still tossing as if in defiance of them. Now he heard the sound of their bolas, cutting viciously through the air. It was a sound that frightened him for he knew what it represented. Within moments his freedom would be lost. They would be upon him.

He made a short run in the direction from which he had come then changed his course, knowing that it was futile. Back he swirled again and even as the gauchos drew near enough to let fly at him with their weapons, the stallion flung himself into the sea, preferring to lose himself among the heavy waters than surrender to man.

The gauchos saw his whiteness dig deeply into the waves which were almost black in colour, reflecting the gloomy sky. For a second his mane and tail were banners, flying freely in the wind, and then the water took them, swirling them about his body. The gauchos cried out involuntarily. The horse would be drowned!

They dragged their mounts to a halt at the edge of the sea and watched in silence as the stallion forged his way through the racing waves. Ahead of him was nothing but a wall of mist, behind him an ever increasing distance between himself and the shore. The gauchos watched until he disappeared, lost in the sea or the mist, or both. They did not know.

'Well, that's the end of him,' remarked one at last, regret in his voice.

The others were silent.

Only when they were sure that the horse would not come up out of the waves again, that the adventure was surely ended as their companion had stated, did they turn their mounts away and return inland.

The beach was lonely again, as ever it had been, and when the men and horses had gone the waves came up over the sand and washed all the hoofprints away.

8 : Aurelio

The turgid mud-brown river turned to silver and gold
when the late afternoon sun touched upon it before
deserting both earth and sky at the end of each day. It was
then that the boy Aurelio liked to slip off his clothes and
slide into it. As its chill waters crept over him until he
felt them lapping gently under his chin he imagined that

he was bathing in a magic river; that the water was the sun's aura and that his thin, tanned body was also touched with gold and silver.

It lasted but a minute, this illusion of his, but it was all he needed to feel that the dirt of the day was cleansed from his body and that with it was washed away his poverty and his dread. The gold and silver filled his pores and gave him anew a sense of hope, a belief in the improbable, an illusion of happiness.

He would come up out of the water when the minute was up and already the river would be mud brown again. Sitting among the rushes and dabbing off the superfluous water with his shirt, it was as though the moment had never happened. Often now the boy's newfound hopes would vanish as rapidly as the silver and gold on the water, as soon as he had pulled on his oft-darned trousers and wrapped the shirt about his shoulders.

There had been a time, when first he discovered the magic of the river, when his illusions would last until he got back home again, often until the following day or longer, but now the circumstances of his life weighed so heavily upon him that they could not be dispelled for more than an instant, and it was difficult to have faith in magic.

It was only because his aunt was ill. It was not the everyday poverty he cared about. He had known nothing else and did not even dream of becoming rich, having no inborn desire to do so. From early childhood he had often entertained himself by staring through the decorated iron grilles that protected the patios of the few rich men of the town. Staring through those bars, which separated the garden from the street, was like staring in upon another world.

The virulent green plants, huge, shining, enticing in their freshness, which the servants dusted and polished much to Aurelio's disbelieving amusement; the roses with blooms of every colour, almost making him giddy with their perfumes; the sparkling fountains with their never-ending source of water; the singing birds that decorated the shadows, and the mosaic tiles which were far too beautiful to be trodden on; all this Aurelio appreciated and admired without wanting any of it for himself. He was happy to know that such a world existed and that he could partake of it, if only from outside in the dusty, unpaved street. He felt that it was as much his as the rich man's and the bars disappeared as he stared because he had no resentment of them.

Sometimes he watched the rich men come out of their small palaces and step into their polished carriages or mount upon glossy, pure-blooded horses, immaculately clothed themselves and their mounts equalling them in grooming and expensive bits and saddlery. Often the rich men, seeing him, would search in their pockets and throw him a coin, which he would recover with dignity, not grovelling like the other lads who sometimes gathered round also.

He was poor, he had nothing material to call his own, but he was not a beggar and had no need of money. So Aurelio had always been content with the shack in which he lived, the straw-packed mattress that was his bed, and the aunt he adored as the only person who belonged to him and loved him.

It was only now, when he was twelve years old, that Aurelio began to feel the weight of his poverty. Now because his aunt was ill and between them they could afford not even the worst doctor in the town to attend

her; now because he knew, although she insistently
denied it, that she would die and he would be left alone.

Oh, it was delicious to sink into the river up to his chin
and for a moment be a child again, lapped by its sun-
touched magic! But the minute he was on the bank,
shivering slightly in the sudden chill of the early evening,
he was no longer a child to be so easily deluded by dreams,
but a boy with the problems of a man upon his shoulders.

II

Aurelio knew that his future was as murky as the river
once the sun was gone. From whence it came and to where
it was going he had no knowledge, and hardly more did
he know about himself. The only realities in his life until
now, apart from his joy in living and his ability to appre-
ciate both simple and beautiful things, had been his aunt
and the adobe hut that had always been his home.

There was a bed; there was a wooden chest containing
a few clothes, most of which had belonged to his mother
and were worn by his aunt. There was one dress, though,
that remained untouched, a dark green velvet, magically
soft to the touch although the years were robbing it of
both its softness and its lustre. This one dress his aunt
refused to wear. It had belonged to Aurelio's mother and
she had worn it on her wedding day. She had worn it
also when she had run away from home. It was the kind
of dress that the wives and daughters of the rich men wore
and Aurelio knew that his mother had suffered poverty
for only a very short time.

Apart from the chest and the bed there was nothing but
a table and two chairs. On the chest, which stood beneath
the one small window that the hut possessed, was a

plaster statue of the one saint his aunt had faith in. Beside
it was a candle, their only illumination at night, for there
was not even a fireplace and the cooking was done in an
oven outside.

Aurelio's aunt was his mother's sister. He called her
Tía Luisa and all that he knew about her, from what she
had told him, was that she had been older than his
mother and as devoted to her as now she was to him.

Sitting on the river bank, hardly noticing how the
water grew darker in the falling shadows of the night,
Aurelio thought of his aunt and his breast swelled with
pain because he loved her so dearly. He knew that she
would be in the house now, waiting for him, probably
lying on the bed and trying to pretend, even to herself,
that her constant weakness was due to the long heat of
the summer days. And he knew that he was a coward
because in spite of his dip in the river he still had not the
courage to return to her and see the incurable weariness
in her features.

Dear Tía Luisa. She had been all to him always. He
had no one else to love. It had always been in her arms
that he found shelter. His mother was dead and his
father. . . . Who knew what had become of his father who
had gone from the house half-crazed with grief and
remorse, never to return. He was almost a wild man anyway, Tía Luisa would try to explain. All the gauchos
were and as uncomfortable living in towns and houses
like ordinary people as would be the savage mustangs
they rode.

'An ill-fated pair were your parents,' Tía Luisa would
say, sighing and blinking the tears from her eyes. Aurelio
knew that she had loved them equally and threw no
blame on his father for all that he had never returned

from his grief-stricken flight from the town.

Then she would explain for the thousandth time how she and her sister had gone to visit the estancia of a friend of their father, and how her sister had fallen crazily in love with an impressionable young gaucho who happened to be working there at the time. They had run away together to be married in some country church miles away from nowhere so that her father could not find them and stop the wedding, and eventually they had come to this town because Aurelio was to be born and his mother wanted to make a home for him.

Aurelio never tired of the story, which was as romantic as anything his imagination could desire.

Tía Luisa had come in spite of a raging father, secretly but urgently as soon as her sister sent for her, and Tía Luisa had stayed to continue what her sister had begun. Aurelio knew that the green velvet dress could have been her dress had she not sold all her finery bit by bit to keep the pair of them alive. Pride had kept her from writing to her family for assistance. She had forsaken it to follow her sister and knew anyway that her father would neither forgive nor understand, and would be capable of leaving the baby in an orphanage, unwanted always.

So Tía Luisa began to do fine embroidery and lace-work for the few gentle ladies of the town but it was a complicated, endless task and earned her very little. She took in coarser sewing, because Aurelio grew and was always hungry, and then the ladies, taking pity on her, offered to let her wash their linen if she promised to be careful with it. There were several offers of marriage in the first years, because she was young and attractive and obviously well bred, but no one wanted the baby and Tía Luisa remained alone.

Now that she was ill and Aurelio's eyes were opened he could understand the many sacrifices she had made for him. He cared so much that it hurt and it hurt because he knew he could do nothing for her in return.

He recalled how she was always busy and often tired. Her once black hair was streaked with grey and on washing days the neat bun she kept it in would fall apart, the hair drooping over her face, sticking to her cheeks and forehead, dark with perspiration. When she was sewing she looked serene and cool, like any grand lady in her parlour, except that she long ago sacrificed her right to such a title and if the sewing were not well done there would be no money to buy food.

When she was not sewing and washing, cleaning and cooking, she even found time to educate Aurelio a little. She taught him to read and write. The only book they possessed was the bible and Aurelio had read it almost from end to end, fascinated by the stories, events and characters unfolded on nearly every one of its fine rice paper pages. She told him stories that she herself had read when younger; she opened his mind to a world that existed beyond the boundaries of this small pampa town, and the rich imagination with which he had been born was succoured by what he read and what he heard, and by what he saw in the jealously guarded patios of the rich men.

Now he knew how he had wasted his days. Instead of dreaming and playing, he should have been caring for Tía Luisa, finding some way of relieving her of her tasks. So often he had made fine promises; how he would look after her when he grew to manhood; and now he was almost a man and still he had done nothing, nor knew what he could do.

Aurelio watched the river, hunching his shoulders as if better to bear the weight that dragged him down. It moved so slowly, so patiently, had always done so and would do so long after he was gone. There seemed to be some kind of message in the river for him if only he could understand it. Perhaps he should follow it one day, find out where it went to. Perhaps where the river ended he would find his destiny.

There was a road that ran alongside the river for many miles, a cart-track deeply rutted by the wheels of the big ox-drawn carts that passed by from time to time. It was the road that all travellers first took on leaving the town. Perhaps his own father had taken this track also to go . . . where?

He could follow that road one day. Perhaps it would take him to his father. Imagination at last won over his problems. He began to smile as dusk settled over the river and the rushes on its banks became thin silhouettes. He would find his father and bring him home to Tía Luisa, and together they would start a new life. Somehow Tía Luisa would be a lady again.

9 : In pursuit of a dream

Had Tía Luisa been well, Aurelio might have set out the very next day on what had suddenly become in his imagination a great adventure. He went home that evening his head racing with visions. For once it seemed that the magic of the river had not failed him and he felt himself capable of anything and everything. But when he reached the hut where he lived, one of a straggling line on the edge of the checkerboard town, his aunt was not outside tending the oven or sewing, as was her wont at this hour, and no glimmer of a candle lighted the doorway.

The boy's heart sank at this reminder of his aunt's illness and the lightness of his body turned to lead as, almost with dread, he approached his home and softly entered.

'Is that you, Aurelio?'

His aunt's voice came from the dark corner and sounded faint.

'Yes, Tía Luisa.'

'Light the candle. It's so dark in here. I must have been asleep and didn't notice how the sun has gone down.'

Aurelio fumblingly obeyed. He was clumsy in his dread, for he was almost afraid these days to see his aunt's face in the candle light, so wan and hollow had it become.

The meagre flame sprang up and sank into a steady glow and shadows moved jerkily on the four rough walls of the hut. Aurelio went over to the bed and sat down beside his aunt, taking one of her hands in his own.

'Where have you been, my son?'

'By the river.'

'You're always by the river. What do you do there?'

'I think.'

'And what do you think?'

'About you. About us. About . . .'

The ideas had suddenly gone from his head. Looking down on Tía Luisa's face, a mere shadow on the pillow, he knew he could not go away and leave her.

'Nothing,' he said. 'Just things.'

Tía Luisa sighed. She stroked the boy's hands that clasped her and said softly, 'Thinking can be painful sometimes.'

'If you were well . . .' began Aurelio, his vision starting up again at the encouraging gentleness of her touch.

'I will get well, Aurelio. This is just a passing ailment. A short rest in bed is all I need.' She paused and then added, 'And what do you think of doing when I'm well?'

'I thought of going to look for my father.'

'Oh, Aurelio!' Disappointment sounded in Tía Luisa's voice. 'But that's only a dream. You're too old now for dreams. How could you ever find him? How would you even know him?'

'If he's alive I would find him. And if I found him, I would know him.'

Aurelio spoke almost violently. Perhaps it was a dream but it was the only one that made life slightly bearable now. But he did not pronounce this thought to his aunt. It would have hurt her too much.

'You must find a job, Aurelio. That's what you need to look for now.'

The boy said nothing. He had tried three different jobs already. With his knowledge of reading and writing, he had been able to find employment as a very minor clerk with three different companies but, with all the will in the world, he had been unable to endure being pinioned to a high stool, copying figures or lists, imprisoned in a musty, paper-crowded room. After a week or so something inside him would explode and he had to leave.

He had to be out in the air, surrounded by space, not walls, and for all the education his aunt had given him, his own character made it worthless to him.

But to cheer her up he said determinedly, 'I will, Tía Luisa. There must be something I can do.'

They smiled at each other in the half-darkness, but

neither was deceived. Tía Luisa knew that Aurelio would not find a job and Aurelio knew that Tía Luisa would not get better.

The woman gently disentangled her hand from the boy's grasp. She waved towards the door.

'Go and heat up the stew,' she said. 'You must be hungry. We might as well eat while we can.'

Aurelio went outside. The fireplace was filled with ashes that were still warm. He added a small amount of fuel, blew up a flame with the help of the candle, and put the earthenware pot over the heat. The stew contained a few chunks of tough cow meat, a couple of potatoes and some rice grains that had sunk to the bottom. The rest was water and spices but it helped to deceive the stomach.

While he waited for the pot to warm through and for steam to rise up from the water, he returned to thinking of the idea that had come to him by the river. Tía Luisa's words returned to him too. 'You're too old now for dreams. How could you ever find him?' Was it only a dream? And even if it were, what else did he have to live on?

II

Tía Luisa survived the wearying heat of the summer and there were even days when she felt quite strong and got through all the sewing that had been left to her as well as some of the washing. People did not leave much washing for her now. She tired rapidly, bent over the big earthenware tub and often had to leave the things unwashed. Then the people would complain because the clothes were not ready when they wanted them and in future sent them somewhere else.

Aurelio earned a few coins writing letters for people

who were too ignorant to write their own but there were not many people in his circle of acquaintances who needed to write at all. He ran errands; he risked his hard-earned centavos gambling on the street corners with the other lads, hoping to augment his income and sometimes succeeding; but always he was haunted by hunger and the knowledge of his aunt's growing weakness.

Tía Luisa also survived the autumn rains and the long damp months of winter. She hardly moved from her bed on many of the days and spoke in a whisper. Half the nights would be spent in coughing when Aurelio would wrap their one blanket tight about her, holding her in fear and agonised love. Their only hope was for the coming of spring, for then the weather would grow more clement and surely Tía Luisa's cough would abate, and she would regather her strength in the sunshine.

Spring came but it came too late to save Tía Luisa. No amount of sun could bring balm to her tortured lungs. She had not the energy to rise from the bed and drag herself to the door to see the fresh blueness of the sky, and even could she have done so the powerful air would have overwhelmed her. Aurelio hung about the house, afraid to leave her. Sometimes the neighbours would come with home-made medicines which Tía Luisa would swallow with difficulty but with gratitude, and the same neighbours would offer the boy a plateful of whatever poor meal they made for themselves.

Sometimes he would go down to the river but now he never saw it change to gold and silver, and the water was cold and gloomy with mud. He would stare at the cart-track and knew that soon, very soon, he would be free to follow it.

Tía Luisa died so quietly one night that Aurelio was

unaware of it until the following morning. The pain in his heart was too hard to allow tears to fall. He knelt beside the bed and held her frozen hand in his own for a long time and was discovered thus by the neighbour who had come with her usual medicine and enquiry. She disentangled the boy from his aunt's side and sent him on various errands to keep him from thinking. By the time the coldness had melted from his heart and he could feel again, Tía Luisa had been buried pauper fashion and he was completely alone.

He wandered about the streets, afraid to return to the house, but when he stopped to gaze through the railings into the rich men's gardens he saw no flowers or singing birds or beautiful tiles. All was a blur to him. His dark eyes were constantly blinded by tears that would not let him focus on anything for all that he wiped them away or let them fall unheeding.

Eventually he found himself at the river and on its bank he passed empty, despairing hours, pulling savagely at the rushes. He was unaware of time or the existence of anything outside himself and the sorrow which overwhelmed him, until the creaking sound of wheels brought his attention to the swaying, overloaded ox-cart that passed him on the opposite bank; the black and white beasts patient of their load and heedless of the driver who prodded them with a cane.

A couple of gauchos rode alongside the cart, which was loaded to overspilling with hides of many colours. Aurelio stared at the gauchos.

It was almost dusk and with their hats pulled low over their bearded faces, hunched in ponchos that came down to their knees, they seemed a part of the drooping-headed horses they rode. The last of the day's sunshine glinted for a moment on the big spurs that were tied to the naked heels of one and the rough, toeless boots of the other.

Something stirred in Aurelio's heart, something deeper and stronger than the sorrow that flooded him. One of these men could be his father. From their kind he himself had sprung, and to them he belonged. Tía Luisa had taught him to read and write. The town itself had tried to form his character to its ways. But always he had been an outsider, incapable of sitting at an office desk, drawn always to the river and the open pampa beyond which had been calling him so subtly that until this moment he had not recognised its call.

The wish to find his father—was that too just part of the call, the gaucho blood that made him uneasy in the town?

Aurelio's heaviness suddenly melted away and with his eyes he could see again. There was a yearning that overcame his heartache for now his destiny was clear.

III

'Yes,' agreed the hostler at the stable in the town. 'I can sell you a horse easily enough.'

He stared at Aurelio, noticing the patches and tears in his clothes, the hungry thinness of his face.

'I can even give you a horse if you like.'

He laughed at the eager light that came to the boy's eyes.

'It's not the horse that costs money, lad. You buy the saddle and bridle and I'll throw in a horse free of charge.' As an afterthought he added, 'I suppose you can ride?'

'Of course,' retorted Aurelio with all the dignity he could muster. It would never do for a prospective gaucho to admit that he had never been on the back of a horse in all his life. 'How much do you want for the saddle and bridle?'

The man told him and Aurelio promised to return just as soon as he had raised the money. Then he went back to the hut in which he had been born, mustered together all the possessions contained within. including the green velvet dress that had belonged to his mother, put them outside and offered them to any interested passer-by.

The amount he eventually collected was pitifully small for there was no one in that district with money to spare for any unnecessary article, and Aurelio returned to the horse-dealer with less than the money he needed.

For a long time the hostler hesitated and Aurelio in his innocence dreaded that he would be turned away. But eventually the man said. 'Well, bearing in mind you're only a lad, and having a fondness for young people and also a generous heart, I'll make a deal with you. You can have the saddle and bridle and also the horse, but of course he can't be as good a horse as I would have offered you. You understand that, I suppose?'

'Oh yes!' cried Aurelio, ready to agree to anything in his eagerness to set out on his great adventure.

The man motioned to the boy to follow him and in the dark corner of a foul-smelling stall Aurelio dimly made out the shadow of a horse.

'That's him. And a bargain for the money you've got. He mightn't be a beauty, and he mightn't be so young, but he's a horse and that's what you're needing.'

The hostler led out the horse, plonking down a dirty, shabby-looking woollen saddle over its back as he did so. In the daylight Aurelio saw that it was astonishingly gaunt and bald in patches. He was too ignorant of horses to notice the rheumy eyes, the sagging quarters and the general ill-appearance of the animal. It was not the splendid animal he had imagined himself possessing, but it was better than nothing and all he could afford for the time being.

'Has it got a name?' he said to the man, unable to think of any complimentary remark or even feel it necessary to thank him.

'Mouse,' said the man, 'and a good beast he is for all that he doesn't look up to much.

He draped a badly mended bridle about the horse's head, pulled up the saddle girth and handed the reins into Aurelio's hands. Meanwhile, Mouse seemed indifferent to all that occurred.

Aurelio handed over the money and, anxious that the hostler should not be aware of his ignorance of horses, preferred to lead the animal down the street and out of sight of the stable before attempting to mount him.

'We make a fine pair, Mouse and I,' thought Aurelio with a grimace, as the horse almost staggered beneath his weight, but his heart was light as the horse plodded along the street, bearing him towards the river and the track that wound its way across the pampa.

Even though Mouse swayed and seemed to have the gait of a cow; even though Aurelio felt uncomfortable in the saddle and hardly knew how to manage the reins that were harsh and too big for his fingers, he was borne up by a sense of anticipation, and excitement burned within him.

He felt no regrets about leaving the town. He had no special friends to say goodbye to or to miss. Ahead of him was freedom, the life of the gaucho that he was determined to make his own, and perhaps—if fate were kind to him—he would also fulfil the dream that Tía Luisa had gently derided.

10 : Santa Clara

Don Jacinto Negrin, owner of the estancia Santa Clara, looked down from his horse at the boy who had asked him for a job. He saw a thin-faced, exhausted lad whose town clothes were dirty and tattered, whose shoes were broken and laceless, loosely holding the reins of a creature he assumed to be a horse and which looked as broken and

tattered and exhausted as its owner. In spite of the boy's
youth and weariness and semi-starved appearance, there
was something about him that spoke in his favour.
Perhaps it was no more than the bright hope that shone
in the dark, hunger-shadowed eyes, and the lack of
humility in spite of the obvious need.

'What's your name?' said Don Jacinto as coldly as he
could. He wanted no beggars or scoundrels on his land.

Aurelio told him.

'And where do you come from?'

Aurelio answered politely, but without forsaking his
dignity in spite of his shabbiness and the scornful look
that the estanciero directed at him.

'Why do you come here looking for work? Have you
run away from home? There's no place here for thieves
or vagabonds.'

'I'm neither one nor the other,' retorted Aurelio, stung
by the man's injustice, and he turned his back on Don
Jacinto, preparing to mount again and look in another
place for a job.

'Wait,' demanded Don Jacinto. 'Don't run off so fast.
This is the only place near here where the dogs are fat
and you'll fare far worse somewhere else. Tell me what
you can do and I'll tell you if there's work for you.'

'Anything,' said Aurelio. 'And what I don't know I'll
soon learn.'

The man liked the spirited sound of his reply. For the
first time he laughed and looked in a kindlier fashion
at the boy.

'Very well then. Go to the kitchen and get yourself
something to eat. You'll find the major-domo there. His
name's Serafin. Ask for him and say I've just employed
you. And make sure you work. The dogs may be fat but

they earn their keep.'

'And so shall I.'

'Colt!' cried the man. 'Wait till you've felt whip and spurs,' but he laughed to himself as he watched the boy walk slowly towards the house, his gait obviously that of one who has ridden too far and is unaccustomed to the saddle.

II

There was nothing grand about the Estancia Santa Clara. Don Jacinto was a bachelor and the adobe hut that had originally been the estancia house was still enough for him. Its three dark rooms were roofed with thatch, its floors were the hard earth over which hens wandered and pecked, fleas and bugs jumped, and dogs sprawled gnawing at bones. There was a rough bed piled with dirty sheepskins on which the owner presumably slept; the middle room contained a few shabby chairs, a wooden chest and some faded prints tacked to the walls, including two pictures of the gaucho president, Rosas; and the third room was the kitchen.

This latter was the friendliest room in the house though no cleaner than the rest. A fireplace fed its flames into a huge chimney and was big enough to roast a lamb or a calf on the spit. There was a long deal table with benches on either side, a few greasy sheepskins scattered about the corners where a gaucho occasionally slept when the weather was inclement, and the smoke-grimed walls offered uncertain refuge to insects of every kind.

This was to be Aurelio's home for the next two years, the place where the fifteen gauchos who worked for Don Jacinto foregathered in the early hours of the morning, hardly before the sun could touch upon the pampa and dispel the mists of spring and summer, to pass round the maté pot and discuss with a few words the work of the coming day.

Some would stay behind to mend a broken bridle or saddle girth, but most of them would be off within minutes of the given order, spurring their half-wild ponies and yelling like Indians to make them buck and rear with flattened ears. Aurelio soon discovered that there was nothing a gaucho liked more than to start the day battling with his horse.

The other gauchos would watch and join in the yelling, sometimes flailing the bucking animal with their own whips to make it fight more, and Aurelio would watch with admiration the skill of the rider who was so much a part of his mount that nothing the latter could do would dislodge him. If only he could ride like that! Then, and then only, would he have the right to call himself 'gaucho' as they did.

He felt an outsider when he watched these early morning displays, for not only was he a very incompetent rider but he did not even have a horse capable of springing two inches from the ground. Poor old Mouse almost collapsed under his weight every time he mounted and one screech from a nearby gaucho was enough to set him trembling.

The other men laughed at Aurelio's Mouse and called the poor brute by many a name but, for all that Aurelio was ashamed of the horse and longed for a better one, he he also knew that he was fond of it and would not have it suffer any ill. This sentiment he kept to himself, of course, for the gauchos ridiculed him enough already in spite of the rough affection with which they had immediately accepted him.

He felt an outsider too because of the clothes he wore,

town clothes for all that they were tattered and fit only for a beggar. He wanted to dress like the gauchos with a pair of long, white cotton pants trimmed with a deep border of lace, and a length of coloured cloth to wind round his waist and between his legs, over the pants, with a belt to keep it from slipping. He wanted a poncho in place of his jacket with its frayed elbows, but there were neither pants, chiripá, nor poncho until he had earned himself some money to pay for them. The major-domo, Serafin, had suggested that he buy these things at the nearest store, in a small village some ten miles away, but he had too much respect for the boy's pride to offer him the loan of a few pesos.

Instead he told him to watch the men when they brought in a cow for killing, so that he might learn to kill and to skin such an animal; to watch the domador, the horse-breaker, with the wild mustangs, to learn his tricks if not his skill. He gave the boy harness to mend, told him to keep up the stock of fuel for the fire, found many a trifle to keep him busy about the house, and Aurelio complied with all that was bade of him, though often he was impatient and sullen because he had not ridden so far to watch other men work and wait on them.

But one day, after he had been at the estancia for about a fortnight, the major-domo said to him, 'There's a bay horse in the corral. Don Jacinto says that it's yours if you can ride it, in payment for the work you've done.'

Aurelio's heart leaped with excitement at these words and he could hardly contain himself from running out to the corral to see the horse. It was becoming an embarrassment to ride Mouse and almost a cruelty, for the poor beast grew weaker in spite of the good grass it was eating and the little effort it was called upon to make.

'Wait!' commanded the old gaucho, smiling at the boy's eagerness. 'I'll come with you.'

The corral was only a few yards away from the house but it ill became a gaucho to walk and so both the major-domo and the boy mounted their respective horses and rode over to it. There was only the bay horse there so that Aurelio could make no mistake, and at first he was disappointed because the animal was as ugly as Mouse, though in much better condition and obviously much younger.

'There he is!' said the gaucho. 'He's only been ridden a few times and so far has no respect for whip or spur. But, in spite of his looks, he's a tough beast and intelligent. He'll make a good mount if you learn how to handle him.'

These were a lot of words from a man who always pondered deeply before opening his mouth, and Aurelio's heart sank as he heard them. This was obviously a joke of the patron's. He looked at the roman-nosed, small-eared bay, which had stopped its eternal pacing about the corral to return the boy's stare with bright but wary eyes.

'Well,' said the gaucho. 'Don't you want him? Have you so many horses that you need no more, even as a gift?'

Aurelio looked at the major-domo, stirred by his sarcasm, but there was a twinkle in the old man's eyes as he said, 'There's no one to see you. I'll help you this first time if you wish.'

The boy nodded. He licked his lips, which had suddenly gone dry, and then he was following his mentor into the corral and watching with envy the ease with which Serafin caught the horse with his lasso and pulled him up to the snubbing post in the centre of the corral.

'Get a saddle on him quickly and cinch him up tight,'

snapped the gaucho, keeping the rope taut.

Aurelio hurried to obey and, aware of Serafin's critical eyes, had no time to think of fear or awkwardness. Somehow he got the saddle on the wild-eyed bay, noticing how it trembled and held itself tight against what it knew would come next.

'And a halter,' called the major-domo.

There was one hanging over the fence. Aurelio approached the horse's head and got the halter round its ears and muzzle.

'Now! Up on its back and hold on with your knees and your hands for all you're worth.'

Aurelio dared not disobey, though his heart was in his stomach and the latter churned almost enough to make him dizzy. He was on the horse's back and the major-domo had slackened the rope that held the bay still. Within the space of half a second Aurelio saw sky and earth and corral bars and the blurred outline of the gaucho on his horse. The hard ground seemed to split every bone, and rocked violently for an interminable period.

The gaucho was saying something but Aurelio could not make out his words. After a while he was aware of the bay horse standing beside him, looking down at him with what appeared to be an expression of amusement. Now he heard the gaucho shouting, 'Up again. Don't waste time. I've work to do.'

Aurelio dragged himself upright and somehow got back into the saddle. But hardly had he tangled his fingers in the horse's mane when once again he was on the ground, stunned and sick and aching.

'Keep at it, boy,' he heard the gaucho say, among the mists that clouded his pounding head, and he blinked the

tears from his eyes, ashamed that the old man should
see them.

III

Aurelio obeyed the major-domo. Every morning he rose
reluctantly from his sheepskin bed and, after partaking of
the hot and bitter maté which was all the gauchos break-
fasted, he took saddle and halter and went to the corral
to begin his daily battle with the bay horse. Serafin no
longer watched or helped but he expected the boy to
obey, and Aurelio knew loneliness and pain, anger and
frustration, when every day the gelding defeated him.

His body was covered with bruises and he could hardly
walk. His hands were swollen and stiff with the cuts that
the horse's wiry mane had sliced into them. But at least
the gauchos forbore from asking him how he progressed
and neither did they make fun of him as was their wont.

Sometimes Aurelio would watch the domador with a
horse brought newly from the pampa and he marvelled
to see how this man could stay astride in spite of all that
the savage, frightened animal could do. If occasionally
he was unseated, or the horse fell, the man never sprawled
disgracefully to the ground as Aurelio did, but landed
always on his feet and was on the horse's back again even
before the animal itself could scramble to all fours. It
looked so easy but Aurelio, sore and aching, knew
otherwise.

He despaired of ever learning to ride the horse and
hated it with a bitter hatred. In the few seconds that he
managed to stay on its back he would punish it with all
his might, flaying its ears and neck and withers with the
whip the major-domo had given him.

Sometimes at night it was hard to restrain the tears that

choked within him, so weary and pain-racked was his body, and then he would think of Tía Luisa and long for the comfort of her arms about him. He would remember only the pleasant times that he had shared with her, and the times that he would swim in the river and the only pain he ever felt was that of hunger; and he wondered why he had ever wanted to be a gaucho, or how he had come to believe that the life they led was romantic and exciting.

It was hard and comfortless and pain-filled and only the poor horse, Mouse, gave him any comfort. Perhaps because in the horse he was reminded of that other life he had left, when he had been a town boy longing for the pampa.

He lost all count of time and place. His world was the bay gelding and his daily battle with it, and there came a time when even the pain of his cuts and bruises faded, so strong was his hatred and his determination to conquer the stubborn animal.

Eventually he succeeded. He never knew how long it took him nor how it happened, but one late afternoon, after he had clung for what seemed an eternity, his head thrown back and forth as if he were a broken-backed marionette, his teeth occasionally biting his tongue, he suddenly felt the fight go out of the animal and he knew he had won.

Now he was the victor and a wild feeling of glory and power surged through him. He thrashed the faltering animal with his whip and for the first time cried out like the gauchos, a shrill excited sound of which he was not even aware.

The horse bucked a few more paces then came to a standstill, head drooping, flanks heaving, no longer caring

what the boy did. Aurelio yanked the gelding's head up
with the reins, stabbed his heels into its flanks, and made
it circle the corral, three, four, five times round, until he
was sure that it obeyed him and knew that he was
master.

Then, utterly weary, the giddy joy of triumph gone, he
almost fell from the horse's back, staggered to the fence
and clung there, retching.

He told no one of his victory but somehow they knew.
Perhaps it was the proud light come newly to his eyes, or
perhaps it was because the major-domo no longer heard
him groaning and suppressing weary sobs in the night.
Still he had not ridden the horse in front of them but all
of them knew that he had mastered it.

One morning, some five or six days later, when he
awoke he found on the floor beside his sleeping place a
pile of clothing. Wonderingly, he took hold of the separate
pieces; a grey woollen poncho with black stripes, a dark
blue length of cloth—the chiripá, and a pair of lace-
bordered pants, stiff with newness. There was even a new
white shirt, a blue neckcloth and a wide leather belt.

The gauchos had left him alone to discover their gift
and for this the boy was glad, for his emotions were
shamefully unmanly. He threw off his town clothes and
donned the others. He even put on the poncho, although
it was not cold. Only his town shoes were out of place and
he kicked them off. Many of the gauchos went barefoot
and so could he.

At last he gathered the courage to go outside. The
gauchos pretended not to notice his new clothes, busy with
their mounts, and Aurelio was glad. He went to the
corral where the horse was waiting for him and began
the ritual of the day, saddling, haltering, mounting.

The horse began to buck and toss as usual but Aurelio, confident in his victory and his new clothes, punished him with the whip and encouraged his wildness. For several minutes the two fighting creatures flung about the corral together and then the boy, over-confident and unsuspecting, found himself sailing through the air and landing with a crash against the corral bars.

For a minute he was completely stunned and came to himself at the sound of hilarious laughter. He shook the dust and dizziness from his eyes and saw that most of the gauchos had watched his performance. Their utter delight at his downfall was almost infantile and for a moment pride and anger surged hotly through him.

He painfully pulled himself to his feet, longing to think of some sarcastic remark to fling at them as he beat the dust out of his new clothes, but their laughter was infectious and soon he too was laughing.

His reaction was greatly appreciated by them and, after a moment, their laughter became whoops and screeches as they spurred their horses and galloped off to work. One of them flung back a remark which completely dispelled any shame that Aurelio might afterwards have felt.

'I thought it was just the clothes that were "gaucho", but it looks as though the body inside them might be gaucho, too.'

Aurelio saw that it was Serafin who spoke and his heart swelled with pride and happiness. He went up to the bay gelding, waiting patiently for him this time and with no great willingness to fight.

'Come on, bicho. I'll teach you who's the boss,' but, as he mounted, he felt something akin to affection for the animal which had, after all, given him a footing into the world to which he wished to belong.

11 : Lessons and legends

In the days before barbed-wire fencing was introduced to the pampa, all the creatures that dwelt there roamed wherever fancy led them. The Estancia Santa Clara had no clearly marked boundaries, except on its southern side where a river divided it from another man's land, and the semi-wild cattle and sheep which bore the brand of Don Jacinto were kept from wandering by the gauchos whose job it was to herd them to new pastures and guard against strays.

For the best part of the year the job was almost a sinecure. There was little to do but circle slowly about the scattered herd, urge on a few laggers, and stop the bulls from killing each other. Some kept guard at night while others slept nearby beside a fire which was built to discourage marauding lions, to roast meat and to boil the kettle for the maté.

The gauchos took with them seven or eight horses, which they changed three times a day, leaving the rest under the guardianship of their bell mare. This latter was usually of light colouring or pinto markings so that she could be found easily in the dark, and she wore a bell round her neck to which the other members of the troup soon became accustomed and which they always followed. Each mare had a bell with a different tone which the troup instantly recognised. The mare was hobbled, but otherwise left to wander at will, and in this manner the gauchos could leave their horses to graze as they pleased without needing to worry about losing them.

When Aurelio was first allowed to ride out with the gauchos to care for the herd he had only two horses, Mouse and the bay gelding which he had named Bicho. At first he had felt pride at possessing two horses when so recently he had had none at all, but soon he realised that two horses were nothing and that a gaucho's pride was in the number of horses he possessed and the fact that all should be similar in colouring. Mouse hardly counted as a horse at all and was of mealy colouring, while Bicho was a bay. Aurelio, slowly realising that most of the gauchos possessed at least thirty horses and never travelled without seven or eight of them, was very soon dissatisfied.

At first, however, he hardly worried about his beggarly position. He and Bicho still had a lot to learn together and it was some time before a whole day spent in the saddle stopped causing him agony. Prestige made him whip up the bay every morning to make him toss and kick in company with the other mounts, though his aching back and muscles cried out against every jerk and occasionally he disgraced himself by being unseated.

Bicho had no more idea of cattle herding than did Aurelio and it was just as well that in the early months there was nothing to do but circle about the herd and keep well clear of the large, savage horns the wild cows shook whenever the shadow of horse or man fell over them. Now and again the major-domo would lend Aurelio one of his horses, partly to give Bicho a rest—for he never even bothered to ride Mouse now and only brought him along for show—and partly because an experienced horse could teach an ignorant rider quite a few things about handling cattle.

The summer went by and Aurelio learned. He learned how to swing the bolas, though was rarely capable of ensnaring an animal. 'Keep at it, boy,' the major-domo would say, and Aurelio kept at it, practising with poor Mouse who came in handy after all and was endlessly patient when Aurelio constantly tangled his legs in the whirling stone balls and leather.

He learned to pick out a cow from the herd and drive her before him without alarming her unduly to the gauchos waiting with their knives to butcher her. He learned how to give signals to his horse with a touch of rein on the neck or the lightest pressure of knees or heels, and was patient with Bicho who was learning too. He learned how to build a fire, how to make the maté, how to skin a beast and prepare it for roasting, and how to eat his meat gaucho fashion, putting a chunk between his teeth and slicing through it with his knife without cutting off his nose. As the knife had a blade some eighteen inches long this was no mean feat.

His new clothes were baptised with dust and sweat and grease but by the end of summer he felt he had the right to call himself a gaucho. He did not say this thought aloud to anyone but it gave him great satisfaction.

Aurelio was not always learning. There were times when he had nothing to do, at the end of the day perhaps when both he and Bicho were released from bondage, the horse to graze and he to throw himself down by the fire to either think or not, as he chose. He would watch the flames burn down to glowing embers and at times a surge of loneliness would come to him for he would be reminded of the oven at his old home and of Tía Luisa.

It was another world, and seemed now as distant as the moon that sailed silently over the earth every night. Aurelio would watch the moon and sometimes wonder at it, and the moon would also make him feel lonely. It emphasised the extreme emptiness of the vast, unending pampa, treeless, almost houseless, going on to an invisible horizon. The crazy widow bird would sob at night and it sounded like the sobs of a desperately unhappy woman. All the gauchos would share Aurelio's loneliness and draw closer to the fire, some glancing about warily in fear of ghosts or bad spirits that were supposed to dwell in those regions at night-time.

One would say that the crazy widow bird was in reality a woman bewitched. 'She was captured by the Indians and taken to live among them, but not until she had seen her husband tortured and killed. So much did she wail and weep that even the Indians tired of hearing her and, to punish her, she was turned into a bird and cast out to eternal loneliness.'

The gauchos stirred uneasily on hearing this tale and there was not one of them that did not believe it for, although they were Christians, they lived too long in the wilderness and among animals to be able to cast off primitive fears and imaginings. Even Aurelio, in spite of the education his aunt had given him, in spite of his twelve years in the town, shivered and half believed. Who could not believe when these fierce, callous, half-savage companions of his crossed themselves and were frightened?

In the mornings, when the embers were stirred to life to heat up the kettle, often before the sun was more than a suspicion of grey light in the still dark east and the moon held sway in the sky, Aurelio would forget his fears and loneliness, stirred by the sharp air, warmed by the companionship of the maté pot which was passed from hand to hand and imbibed through the same silver tube. Hardly anyone spoke at that hour of the day and the only noises were those of the horses that whickered to greet the advancing dawn, or a cow lowing softly to a hungry calf. It was a good time of day, fresh, clean and bracing, when spirits no longer wandered and God lighted up the world with His glory.

II

Aurelio had not forgotten his original reason, reached at the riverside over what seemed an eternity ago, for coming to the pampa. He was determined to find his father, even if it meant relating his tale to every single gaucho he ever met, but at the beginning he was too much a nobody, too unproven to expect their attention to anything he said. He was even too shy to speak boldly of a subject so close to his heart. And then he had been too busy learning, so tired and so often aching, to even notice how the time went by and his only thoughts had been of Tía Luisa.

But by the time his new clothes were as shabby-looking as those of his companions and he had Bicho more or less educated as well as himself, when he felt that he was an accepted member of the company and knew that their affection for him was sure-founded, then did Aurelio speak of his father and ask the gauchos if they knew anything of him.

He hardly expected to be successful in his search from the beginning and it was as well for, although the gauchos sought back in their memories, none of them could recall a man who might have been Aurelio's father, not even Serafin who was older than the rest and had travelled from one end of the pampa to the other.

'Perhaps he went over to the Indians,' suggested the old gaucho. 'It's the only place where a gaucho not wanting to be found can successfully hide.'

'But why should he want to hide?' asked Aurelio.

The idea of a man living voluntarily among the Indians was beyond him. He had as yet seen none but a few in the town, domesticated Indians who had been captured in battles and made slaves by their captors. They were called servants but in reality they were slaves and had come to the town in cages, like wild animals.

Every civilised person was afraid of the Indians and many of the ranchos and estancias were surrounded by moats or wide ditches to keep them at bay, with a look-out

tower and even a cannon with which to fight them. The
Indians were masters of diabolic tortures and were as
cruel to their own race as to the Christians. The fact that
most of the gauchos had Indian blood was overlooked by
them, and the gauchos were the Indians' greatest enemy,
almost as savage as they were and as skilled in horse-
manship, lance-throwing and hand-to-hand killing.

'If a man disappears for twelve years,' replied the
major-domo, 'the chances are that he went over to the
Indians. Otherwise he would have turned up again,
sooner or later. Perhaps they murdered him, or perhaps
they accepted him and he was killed off by one of their
diseases or the foul medicines they make to cure them.'

A gloomy death was the most satisfactory end to any
story, as Aurelio was to learn, and none of the gauchos to
whom he spoke on the subject could proffer him any
better suggestion.

Aurelio asked the horse-breaker, for he was a man who
travelled from place to place and brought all outside news
to the estancia, but even he could tell Aurelio nothing.
So for the time being the boy was no nearer to com-
pleting his mission.

Meanwhile, the seasons passed. Aurelio continued to
learn. There was the branding of the new calves in spring
time and the occasional wearisome treks to some town,
driving a herd of two or three hundred head of cattle to
its stockyards and slaughterhouses.

The first such trip came for Aurelio in mid-winter and
if he thought he had learned all there was of enduring and
suffering, he discovered that he was mistaken. The trip
took a fortnight to complete and it rained every day of
the fourteen. They could light no fires at any stopping
place and their clothes clung to them, frozen and soggy,

and even the woollen poncho could not keep out the wetness that fell unceasingly from the sky, or protect his face from hailstones, or his hands from freezing. They lived on strips of tough beef, which was cured in the manner of the Mongols, by putting the crude meat between the horse and the saddle, leaving the salt that was sweated from the horse to do the curing.

Aurelio's only consolation was that the other gauchos, for all that they were seasoned, suffered as much as he, perhaps more stoically, but even custom could not make the change from summer to winter more agreeable.

The second trip he would have avoided if he could, but the major-domo was determined to make a gaucho of him as soon as possible and insisted that he rode along, even if it were only to round up the stragglers. With Bicho his only mount, he could not afford to overwork him, but it was on the second trip that Aurelio gained himself another horse.

There was a cock-fight in the town and he, with his companions, their work completed, went to watch. The gambling was as wild as the excitement, though Aurelio found little pleasure in the spectacle, still not accustomed enough to brutality and death to accept it as a natural sequence. However, his emotions were stirred enough for him to defend the losing cockerel recklessly, offering Bicho as security for his bet, and for some reason fate was kind to him. His cockerel won and almost dazed with disbelief he found himself with the choice of a gaucho's string of ponies.

Serafin came with him to make sure that he was not deceived and, on his advice, Aurelio picked out a strong-looking bay, smaller than Bicho but prettier, which the old gaucho promised was the best of the troup. He was no doubt right, too, if the loser's face was anything to judge by when Aurelio had made his choice.

So the boy went back to Santa Clara rejoicing, in spite of the rain, the cured beef and the coldness. He rode the new pony to give Bicho a rest and the grey, waterlogged pampa seemed a beautiful place.

12 : The hunt

Most of the gauchos worked only long enough to earn themselves a few silver pesos and then, as swiftly as they had come, they were gone, to spend their money on new clothes, a new knife perhaps, gambling in the town and in other diversions. When the money was gone they would go in search of another job, but they were too wild and independent to stay at one place for more than a few months. Only a few stayed on, the old ones like the major-domo who had done his share of roaming and to whom the temptations of the town no longer appealed, and the married ones who had a wife and several children living on the estancia land.

Sometimes when a gaucho was leaving Santa Clara he would ask Aurelio if he wanted to go along but the boy always shook his head. For the time being he was content to stay where he was, in the place where he had found affection.

Once, when Serafin heard the boy turn down such an invitation, he said to him, 'You can go along if you wish. It's all learning and you can always come back here when you've had enough or when you've spent your money.'

Aurelio shook his head and smiled at the old man. He was still not gaucho enough yet to want to roam and felt no sense of bondage although for nearly a year he had worked at Santa Clara.

Just as gauchos kept leaving, new ones came, and to all Aurelio put the same question about his father. Most of them shook their heads. Once a grizzle-bearded fellow said that he vaguely remembered some such story of a gaucho running off with the daughter of a rich man, but he did not know how the story ended or what had become of either of them. Neither could he recall where first he had heard the story, nor even if it were true.

During the spring branding the major-domo killed a wild mare. He was in need of a new pair of boots and these he made for himself by pulling off the mare's 'socks', from knee to fetlock. The rest of her carcass he left for the carrion birds and wild dogs, and it was not until he had finished removing the skin he wanted that he discovered the colt that had been running with her. It was little more than a yearling and he pulled it down with his bolas before it could escape. Finding it uninjured, he took it back to Aurelio as a present.

'It's too young to be useful now. You can either keep it or release it as you please,' he said.

Aurelio decided to keep it, for he was anxious to make up his troup of horses as quickly as possible. It was a khaki-coloured beast, with black points and a small white star on its forehead. He hobbled it and left it to graze with old Mouse, who still came along with his master on all his journeys although he was never ridden and continued to be nothing but a bag of bones.

Serafin also captured two more colts for the boy, both almost adult animals and strong enough to be ridden. So again began for Aurelio the bone-jerking daily battle he had first experienced with Bicho, fighting the colts into submission. By summer he had four riding horses, apart from Mouse and the yearling, a small but satisfactory number of silver pesos stowed inside his belt, and the belief that he could truly number himself among the gauchos.

This confidence in his skill was due to his age. He was soon to discover that, for all he could now stay with a bucking horse for several minutes at least, and was handy at cutting out a cow or calf from the herd, he still had much to learn.

When the gauchos had nothing to do, one of their favourite pastimes was practising with the bolas and they would take it in turn to throw them after one another's galloping horses. The major-domo knew by the brightness of the boy and the boldness with which he spoke that he

considered himself a man among other men and, partly
because he thought a lesson in humility would do him
no harm and also to save him from ridicule among
gauchos less friendly than those who knew him, he told
Aurelio one morning to mount his swiftest horse and see
if he could escape the bolas he would swing after him.

The horse he had won at the cockfight, Lucero, was
his swiftest and Aurelio sprang to the saddle with a yell,
so that the horse was already galloping even before he
had his toes in the stirrups. He felt the wind against his
eyes, whipping the breath from his throat. . . . It lasted
but a second for in an instant Lucero turned a somersault
and he was flung to the ground, jarring his shoulder
horribly. He had travelled no more than fifty yards.

He heard the watching gauchos laugh as he pulled
himself to his feet, then set about untangling the bolas
from the bay's kicking hindlegs so that he also could rise.
He felt angry with the major-domo for having made a
fool of him, and he gasped as he pulled the bolas loose for
his wrenched shoulder pounded with pain.

Serafin rode up and held out his hand for the bolas.
He saw the flash of anger in the boy's eyes and said
implacably, in a voice loud enough for the others to hear,
'A gaucho would have landed on his feet.'

II

One day some Englishmen came to Santa Clara to speak
with Don Jacinto. Aurelio had never seen gringos before
and he watched them with undisguised curiosity.

'What do they want with the patron?' he asked the
major-domo.

The old man knew for they had come before. 'They're

traders in hides and feathers and horse hair. You'll see. In a few days' time Don Jacinto will send us all hunting and we'll fill up two or three ox-waggons with skins for the gringos.'

So it was. All but a few of the gauchos set out on their best horses, checked to see that their tack was in good condition, sharpened their knives and made themselves extra sets of bolas. Hunting and killing were the gauchos greatest pleasures and, for all that Aurelio had not yet learned to be bloodthirsty as they were, even he caught the general excitement and was as eager for the chase as his companions.

They set off one early morning before the stars had faded from the sky and the pampa was still covered with darkness, charging across it in a horde of pounding hooves and wild shrieks. Aurelio was riding Bicho and his heart thrilled almost with fear as he found himself caught up in the centre of these wild men, knowing instinctively that Bicho was feeling the same, for the bay gelding raced as he had never raced and his eyes were wild, his ears flattened against his skull.

As dawn came, and long before they were in sight of any game, the gauchos were already letting fly with their bolas, aiming at birds on the wing, startled up from their nests among the hummocks. Plover and peewits fell, crushed by the spinning balls and leather and, as they touched the ground, the gauchos leaned from the saddle and grabbed them up, their mounts not faltering or slackening in speed. Aurelio saw and marvelled at such dexterity and the reproof of the major-domo, which until then still smarted, suddenly seemed just to him.

When the first flush of excitement faded the gauchos drew their mounts to a halt. The ox-drawn carts were far behind them and would not know of their whereabouts if they continued in such a manner. They exchanged horses and a few words of conversation, and some stayed on the spot to wait for the waggons while the rest went on in search of wild horses, a herd of guanacos or a flock of rheas.

Aurelio was among those who stayed behind, for he had no skill as a hunter, and he chafed at the wasted morning, waiting for the waggons, knowing that somewhere in the distance his companions were enjoying themselves. At last the waggons came, the red-and-white oxen strolling doggedly along, heedless of the driver who poked at them with a long cane and urged them faster. There were three teams of six oxen each and Aurelio helped to unyoke them to let them graze while they awaited the return of the hunters.

Eventually they came and their hands and clothes were spattered with blood. They had encountered a small herd of wild horses which they had captured and killed on the spot. The oxen were yoked again to follow the still excited gauchos to the place of the killing, and when they reached it Aurelio's eagerness suddenly died.

For what seemed an interminable distance the pampa was covered with the corpses of horses that had died violently and the earth was soaked red all about them. Already chimangos, the pampa hawk, were circling in the wind currents or stalking about on the ground near and around the bodies.

The gauchos were unperturbed by the scene and immediately set to work to skin the animals they had killed. It was a long and wearisome task for there were some three hundred horses lying there. A knife was put into Aurelio's hand and he was supposed to help with the work but he stumbled from corpse to corpse, seeing the lifeless eyes staring skywards, the heavy-maned necks stretched out, the jaws drawn back in a frozen whinny of terror and pain, until they haunted him and he could not bring himself to lay a hand upon them, let alone hack off their tails.

The next day the gauchos fell upon a flock of rheas. Aurelio was among them this time and he learned why the gauchos referred to this bird as the most 'gaucho' of all the pampa dwellers, for in astuteness it was next to the gaucho himself and no easy prey to catch. Just as the hunter was within reach of it and about to swing his bolas, the rhea would twist back on its tracks with such rapidity that, even before the gaucho could realise it, it was behind the horse instead of in front of it. While the gaucho wasted time checking his mount's mad career and turning about, the rhea had made good its escape. It was also the swiftest of creatures, capable of outrunning the freshest horse, and it needed all the gaucho's skill, cunning and patience to entrap it.

Some seventy birds were brought down that morning, the rest escaped, and Aurelio himself did nothing but chase half-heartedly after those he grew close to, swinging the bolas but not releasing it from his grasp. There was more blood, and plenty of feathers for women's hats, which would fetch a good price in the city.

The hunters scoured the pampa for fifteen days before setting a homeward course and then the three big waggons were heavy with multi-coloured hides, big bundles of horse hair, and stacks of soft, plumy feathers. The men were contented, the lust to kill gone out of them, and with some thousand horses dead on the pampa behind them they were still capable of singing with all sincerity, 'My horse was my life, my welfare, my only treasure.'

The major-domo rode alongside Aurelio. He knew of the boy's unhappiness without needing to enquire. He waited for Aurelio to speak, giving him a chance to pour out the sickness that was in him, but Aurelio said nothing, afraid of the man's ridicule. He had come to the pampa wanting to be a gaucho, he had prided himself on his ability, but the boy who had delighted to gaze upon the flower gardens in the rich men's houses could not stomach the sight of so much slaughter.

For hours they rode side by side, Serafin seemingly half-asleep on his pony. Aurelio gazed steadfastly ahead and occasionally jabbed at his mount with his heels when memories became too hard for him and could not be kept at bay. After a while the major-domo gave up. He sighed, spurred his horse forward, and took up his position at the head of the column, But three words he said to Aurelio before he left him, to let him know that he sympathised and understood without condoning.

'Get hard, boy.'

III

Don Jacinto was well pleased with the results of the gauchos' labours and on the day that the gringos returned to Santa Clara to discuss prices, he told the major-domo to arrange a fiesta. Cows and a few sheep were killed for the barbecue, the married men rode in haste for their wives and children, while some of the others went in search of their sweethearts to bring them to the dance that was scheduled for the evening.

Don Jacinto talked business with the Englishmen and the gauchos engaged in equestrian sports, which were for the most part both primitive and dangerous. Aurelio was unable to partake of these for he would have assuredly been killed, but there were horse races in which he dared to match his Lucero against the others. He found, though, that swiftness was not enough and that trickery was not only permitted but expected, so that Lucero came last in every race and again it was shown to him that, for all he could judge himself a good rider by city standards, he was still only a beginner among the gauchos.

The roasted meats were attacked with gusto and chunks were thrown generously to the dogs that hung about hopefully, and in the afternoon a turgid silence fell over the men and the dogs and the horses, all tired and replete. But Aurelio could not doze easily, in spite of the good meat he had eaten and the wine he had drunk.

Somewhere near a gaucho was softly recalling the ballad that began, 'My horse was my life, my welfare, my only treasure,' and it brought back too vividly all that he was trying to forget of the last few weeks. He had seen Don Jacinto and the Englishmen haggling the whole morning over the price for the skins and feathers, while on the pampa the hawks and wild dogs would still be gorging on the wasted carcasses. One day, he supposed, a storm would wash the blood away.

13 : Land of mists

During the following autumn the major-domo told Aurelio that he was leaving the estancia to go on a cattle drive that would take some three months to complete.

'Don Jacinto has some land to the south, a miserable country for sure. It's overrun with cattle, some branded and some not. We only go down there once every three or four years, to brand the new stock, kill off the worst diseased ones and choose the best of the bunch to take to the city. Only six of us are going, so it will be hard work. If you want to come along, you're welcome.'

Aurelio eagerly agreed. He was beginning to tire of Santa Clara at last. The work was routine and monotonous, now that he could perform it reasonably well, and this sounded like an adventure at least and would give him a chance to see a bit of the world.

'Don't deceive yourself,' warned the old gaucho. 'It's not country like this. It's along the coast and there's hardly any grass. It's all sand, hills of it as far as the eye can see—which isn't far, for sure, because thick mists cover the land best part of the year. And the cattle aren't like the ones you know. They're wild, with monstrous horns and devilish natures. What with the sand-dunes and the mist you can hardly see them until they're on top of you, and it's a miserable place to die.'

'I'm not afraid,' replied Aurelio.

'No, I don't suppose you are. But remember, I've warned you. It's no place for novices. You can come along but you'd better leave the big cattle alone. There'll be enough for you to do, helping with the branding and the calf-cutting.'

The six gauchos and Aurelio set out from the estancia some three days later. Aurelio left Mouse behind on this trip and took only Bicho, Lucero and the two new geldings. Contrary to custom, none of the men seemed very cheerful at the outset of the journey. They rode with fixed, implacable expressions, and in silence. The only sound was the discordant jangling induced by the movements of the six bell-mares.

'What's the matter?' Aurelio asked Serafin. 'Are we

going to a funeral?'

'Perhaps. I told you it's a miserable place. Apart from the cattle, the only beings that inhabit it are ghosts and bad spirits. You can hear them moaning and howling at night and even during the day. And sometimes, in the night, you can feel them touching your face.'

II

The gaucho had not exaggerated his description of the country into which they eventually rode. The seven riders huddled up in their ponchos and pulled down the brims of their hats. Even Aurelio, in spite of his boyish enthusiasm, felt the oppressiveness of the atmosphere and grew as silent as the rest. It had taken them three weeks to come down to this God-forsaken coastland and the horses trod it unwillingly. The good pampa grass was left behind and here there was only gorse and reeds and a dry, salty grass that was strange to their palates.

The wind blew in from the sea and the air was thick with salt and dampness. Aurelio felt as clammy and uncomfortable as if he had ridden for days through a rainstorm. The sound of the sea, sighing in the distance, disturbed his imagination. Were these the spirits of which the major-domo spoke, already acknowledging their advent?

The sky was grey and in the early mornings the sun shone in an orange ball through the mists. It was never seen in its entirety but always as a blurred stain above them. The horses expressed their dislike for the new terrain by blowing often through their nostrils. Their eyes were white-ringed and their ears flattened against their skulls.

When it was necessary to stop and make camp, none of the horses wandered far from the men. They kept within sight of the fire, bulky shadows on the outskirts of the flickering light, and the bells of the mares sounded hollowly in the gloomy darkness. The gauchos drew close and hardly spoke. All were constantly listening for unexpected sounds. There was not one who doubted the existence of malevolent spirits and now and again one or another would pull out the medallion worn on a chain round their necks, kiss it and mutter a short prayer. They slept with their heads pointed in the direction in which they were travelling for in the grey, blurred light of day the countryside had no distinguishing marks.

Once they came right on to the beach itself, a long, wilderness of beach, with driftwood and seaweed blackening the waves as they ran up to the sand. The horses trod the strange ground almost fearfully and Aurelio was spellbound by his first sight of the grey sea. In a way it was like the pampa, flat, unchanging and endless, the only difference being that the sea was alive, its surface in constant turmoil, and the waves came up like crested, tossing horses, as savage and as unconstrained.

The sea disappeared into a misty distance and Aurelio, alone on the sand with his horse—for the others had ridden ahead and left him to his gazing—was overwhelmed by a sensation of emptiness and was suddenly afraid.

He jerked his horse round and set him at a gallop after the others, and he was glad when they left the beach behind to follow a rough trail which wound through sand-dunes and led them eventually to a rancho, inhabited by a shepherd and his wife. There they stopped the night, at the shepherd's insistence, for so rarely did he see strangers that he could not let them ride by.

Aurelio was glad to be inside a house again, warmed by the heat of a log fire and the light it gave flickeringly to the room. It was a big room, with several dogs sharing the floor-space that was allotted to them for sleeping. The shepherd butchered a sheep and his wife attended to the cooking of it. The gauchos for once grew voluble as they asked questions of the shepherd or replied to those put by their hosts.

On the following day they reached their destination, a deserted ranch-house to which the gauchos gave life when they had thrown down their belongings and set about stirring up a fire. The walls were damp and the roof broken in places, letting in the mist which filtered through the rafters. The horses were put to graze, the sheep which the shepherd had presented to them was killed and jabbed on the spit in the fireplace, and while they ate the major-domo outlined the work that was expected of them.

Aurelio discovered that he was indeed only to help with the branding and calf-cutting and, as he now considered this almost a child's job, he was not very pleased. He had worked hard with his horses all the summer, teaching them the tricks they needed to know, and he wanted an opportunity to try out both their skill and his own. These wild cattle represented a challenge and now it seemed he would not have the opportunity to meet it.

Serafin read the boy's thoughts and his last words before they settled themselves comfortably on their sheepskin saddles for sleep were meant to crush them.

'Remember, boy. Leave the bulls and the big cows alone.'

III

For several days Aurelio worked with efficiency but impatience at his allocated job. He was ready with the branding-irons and the cutting knife whenever a calf was brought, and he envied the gauchos who returned to the base every two or three hours to change horses and to speak briefly of the cattle they hunted.

'Every one is possessed of a devil,' said one gaucho, and he showed the boy the great gash across his mount's breast where a horn had gouged into it. 'My best horse, too,' he added.

Once such evidence might have deterred Aurelio from attempting his skill with the wild cattle, but he had grown fearless as his confidence increased and considered that the accident was due to bad luck, or the fact that working in the mist made things difficult. He was certain that with Bicho or Lucero to aid him he could easily cut out the calves from the herd and afterwards try his skill with something bigger. But he said nothing to the major-domo, knowing that Serafin would not give him permission.

At the end of a week the major-domo called a rest. In the old corral that had been built near the house some twenty years earlier, there were already more than sixty bullocks. Aurelio went to look at them and found them inferior beasts, most of their weight being in the huge horns they carried, for they were skeleton-thin and wiry. He had never seen such animals on the pampa, where there was grass and flowers and alfalfa in abundance so that the animals grew fat and lethargic. He could not imagine why Don Jacinto troubled with them. And these were the best of the herd! He was curious to know what the others looked like.

As it was a day of rest and each man busied himself as he chose, some mending broken harness, some passing round the maté pot and talking desultorily, Aurelio decided to take a horse and wander about on his own to see if he could find some of these dangerous bulls that the gauchos spoke of and which so far he had not seen.

He had grown accustomed to the strange climate, with its mists that rarely lifted, its dampness, and the salt that clung to his skin, but still the atmosphere perturbed him and he longed for the fresh winds of the pampa and its skies of blue and white.

He was riding Bicho and it was pleasant to be alone for a while. A sense of excitement, mingled almost with dread, was tingling through him for he knew in his heart, without actually admitting it, that if he encountered any of the wild cattle he would try his skill with them. He did not intend to actually look for them but if he found them . . . He touched the bolas that was wound about his waist, growing in confidence at the feel of it.

Silence wrapped itself about him. He could hardly even hear the sound of Bicho's hooves, so thick was the ground with wind-blown sand. He rode with the reins slack and Bicho grazed as he wandered along, snatching at the salty grass with distaste but hunger. Now and again the mist lifted and he could see for quite a distance, and at other times it seemed to drop like a blanket over everything and he was aware only of the sand-dunes.

Then, when least he expected it, he came across a whole bunch of the wild cattle, grazing in a hollow. He jerked his horse to a stop to gaze at them and, as he looked from one to another, he realised that the sixty in the corral were in reality the best of the lot for these were the most revolting and monstrous animals he had seen, belonging in truth to this nightmare country. Their bodies were covered with maggot-ridden sores; their horns were deformed and grew into their eyes; some dragged broken limbs, and all were as gaunt as empty wine-skins. Even the fresh-blooded calves could not escape the curse of their birthplace for they were pitiful, rickety beasts, abandoned to the harshness of nature.

All at once, almost in front of him and at hardly more than a hundred paces, a bulky shadow appeared in the mist from behind a sand-dune. By the wide expanse of horn, which was surely too heavy for that paper-thin body to support, Aurelio was in no doubt as to his adversary. For a moment he was taken aback, so suddenly had the beast appeared, and then he saw how it tore at the ground with its hoof and lowered the impossibly long horns with a menacing twist.

Aurelio began to back Bicho away, then he remembered his intentions and hurriedly pulled the bolas into his hand. The bull advanced almost imperceptibly, not decided yet on whether it should attack or no, and Aurelio recalled his lessons and drew Bicho away. The bull was too close, dangerously so, and gave him no room for manœuvres.

Bicho's head-tossing retreat decided the bull. With another shake of his almost prehistoric horns, he came after the horse and rider. With a yell, Aurelio dug his heels in the pony's flanks and Bicho fled, the bull in close pursuit. Aurelio zigzagged as much as the dunes would let him, until the bull fell off his tail, and then he turned about, ready to chase in his turn.

But the bull had no fear and, instead of racing away from his pursuer, he whirled in his tracks and came after Aurelio again. The boy was disconcerted by the bull's swiftness and unexpected behaviour. Bicho's own instinct of self-preservation saved them. The bay gelding hastily side-stepped the charging animal and the left horn missed him by millimetres. Again the bull turned. He was fast in spite of his top-heavy horns and Aurelio had no time to swing the bolas with any effect in the short space and time available to him.

He pulled the horse round and spurred him away, needing more space, but he had forgotten the difficult terrain. This was no flat grassland for easy running and leisurely manœuvres. Bicho lost ground as his hooves sank constantly into the sandy earth and then he slipped against a sand-dune and almost floundered.

The bull was upon them as Aurelio jerked his pony up. He saw the brindle head and the blood-red eyes and, even as Bicho struggled, he felt the gelding being lifted beneath him.

The horse screamed as Aurelio flung himself from the saddle. He landed in a crouched position on the side of the dune. In the same second he was aware of the sand giving softly under his feet, the rank smell of his fear-sweating horse, and the grunts of the savaging bull. Then a heavy weight collapsed on top of him and the grey day turned black.

14 : The parting

When Aurelio opened his eyes he thought he was dreaming. He was in a room illuminated by firelight and could vaguely make out the shadow of the roof with its smoke-blackened beams, the smudged uneven walls, and the figure of a shawl-shrouded woman sitting near him. It was Tía Luisa, and all that was in his memory had been a dream.

He went to sit up and call to her, but the call became a gasp of pain and he fell back again on the sheepskins. The beams and the walls spun. The woman had risen to her feet and, when she no longer spun with her surroundings, Aurelio realised that she was not Tía Luisa at all though her face was familiar.

'Lie still,' came the soft command.

Weakly Aurelio asked, 'Where am I? What's happened?'

'Don't you remember?'

Slowly, Aurelio forced his memory. 'You're the shepherd's wife? . . . A bull attacked me. . . . My horse! What happened to my horse?'

'It's dead and so is the horse of the major-domo. He saved you, or you'd be dead too.'

Aurelio moved his head restlessly. He could remember nothing more than Bicho's terrible scream, the soft sand and the snorting bull. How did the major-domo come to be mixed up in it?

'Don't move,' commanded the woman. 'You've crushed most of your ribs, so be still.'

There was nothing else the boy could do, for the slightest breath he took made him dizzy with pain. He was strapped from his chin to his waist in sheepskins and any movement was impossible. He closed his eyes and let the pain sweep over him, too weak to resist it. Later he was aware of the woman trying to push some liquid between his lips.

'It's a pain-killing herb I've brewed,' she explained as she saw his eyes open. 'Swallow.'

Aurelio obeyed and soon he was drifting into a world of dreams again, of Tía Luisa and green patios, the major-domo and his screaming horse.

How long he lived in this shadowy world of pain and

dreams Aurelio did not know. One day he came out of it and, though the pain was still there, it was bearable. He watched the woman going about her work in the house, tending the fire and the meals, bent over her sewing in the afternoons, and she made him think constantly of Tía Luisa, for she attended him with gentleness in spite of the abruptness of her speech.

Now and again a gaucho would call in to see how he progressed but the major-domo did not come and Aurelio was too ashamed to ask for him.

One day he demanded of a gaucho, 'What happened? Tell me what happened. I don't remember anything.'

'I only know what the major-domo told us,' said the gaucho to whom he spoke. 'That he followed you because he guessed what you were up to. He lost you in the mist and it wasn't until he heard your horse screaming that he discovered you again. He drove at the bull but it was mad with lust and wouldn't leave the horse alone, and you were crushed underneath it. He grabbed the bull by the tail to pull it off-balance and then the bull went for him, too. He drew it away, chasing round the sand-dunes.'

The gaucho paused and then cried, 'It was all the fault of the accursed mist! The bull disappeared and although he wandered around in search of it, it had vanished like a spirit in the night.'

'Then what happened?' demanded Aurelio, almost fearfully, the nightmare memory of the day and the monstrous bull returning.

'He went back to free you from the horse and while he was doing so the bull was suddenly in front of him again with murder in its eyes. His horse shied away in fear and the bull went after it. Its legs got tangled in the reins and it fell. The major-domo carried you back to the camp and then we brought you here to be looked after by the shepherd's wife.'

'And the bull?' said Aurelio.

'The major-domo took another horse and went in search of it. He was angry, angrier than I've ever seen him, because it was his favourite horse that he lost. When he came back half the day had gone by and we were beginning to be afraid for him. But he'd found the bull and broken its neck with his own hands.'

The gaucho stopped for a moment, then continued almost wonderingly. 'We couldn't believe it until we went to see. But it was true. It lay there with its head all twisted and there wasn't a drop of blood on it, except from the horses.'

II

While Aurelio lay helplessly on his back, the days passing slowly and the nights pain-filled, he thought often of the major-domo and his manner of killing the bull. His vivid imagination could picture the scene, the grey-bearded old gaucho with his hands on the bull's horns, dragging it down and down in his rage until, with a final jerk, it was subjugated for ever. The dead horse had been his pride and joy and he had loved it as only a man can when he has neither wife, nor children nor brothers.

Worse than the pain of his broken ribs, was the realisation that Serafin would probably never forgive him for his disobedience and for unwittingly causing the death of his horse. The major-domo never came to the shepherd's house and Aurelio was heavy-hearted. His fondness of the man was second only to the love he had borne for Tía Luisa.

His foolishness had cost him the old man's respect and affection and also his horse, Bicho. He had been fond of Bicho, too, and recalling the time when he had fought the bay gelding in the corral at Santa Clara, and the major-domo's encouragement, the tears came to his eyes. This was indeed an accursed land that had lost him in the same hour both friend and pony.

While the boy pondered and grieved in the shepherd's home, the gauchos finished their work with the wild cattle. They had some four hundred animals to drive back to the estancia and they were glad to go. Winter was approaching. The mists were growing heavier and the nights were frozen.

On the last day the major-domo finally came to see Aurelio. He made no mention of the boy's accident, except to say in his usual undemonstrative manner, 'If you're well enough to sit a horse you'd better come with us.'

Nothing more would Aurelio have desired but he was hardly able to lift himself from the sheepskin rug on which he lay and could never have endured the long journey back to the pampa.

'I can't,' he replied.

'Then we shall have to go without you. The work's finished and we can't stay here any longer. When you're better you'll be able to find your own way back, unless you decide you like it down here. Ride northwards and one day you'll reach the pampa.'

Aurelio nodded. He was afraid to speak for he knew his voice would come out in a sob.

'Your horses are outside,' added the other.

Aurelio nodded again.

'Well,' said Serafin. There was a silence between them

while they stared at each other. 'Well,' he said again. 'We're off.'

'Go with God,' Aurelio forced himself to reply.

The major-domo walked over to the door. He stopped in the entrance and looked back at Aurelio.

'And when you're better . . . don't go playing 'gaucho' any more. You can't afford to crack your ribs a second time.'

'What must I do then?'

This time the sob escaped and, although he pretended not to hear it, the old gaucho relented a little.

'There's a legend hereabouts. The man who can find and ride the sand stallion will be the most "gaucho" of them all.' He grinned at the boy and added, 'You'd better look for him. Whether he exists or not, I don't know. But at least he won't have horns.'

And then he was gone. Aurelio heard his yell and the startled pounding of his horse's hooves. He listened to the rhythmic movement of them over the earth until they grew fainter and fainter and finally disappeared. There was a great emptiness in the boy's heart and the pain of his emptiness was greater than any that his broken ribs had caused him.

Later, when the woman came to ask him if he were hungry, he turned his face to the wall so that she should not see the tears that stained his cheeks.

15 : The sand stallion

Aurelio knew that the gaucho had spoken in jest when he mentioned the sand stallion and that he should search for it, but, having nothing to do but lie on the ground and think, the idea soon took hold of his imagination. He asked the shepherd if he knew of the legend.

'The sand stallion?' said the shepherd. 'Yes, I've heard

of him. It's a white stallion that's supposed to live in these parts, but it must be just a legend as I've never seen him.'

'And how old is the legend?' Aurelio wanted to know.

The shepherd shrugged his shoulders. 'It must have started some six or seven years ago. The gauchos who come down here began saying that they had seen a beautiful white stallion which when chased always disappeared into the sea. But to my mind it was just the mist that deceived them.'

'Is that all?' said Aurelio. It seemed very little.

The shepherd hesitated and then continued, 'Once, when I'd been laughing at the gauchos for chasing after this will-o'-the-wisp, they took me with them to where they'd last seen it, a long distance off, in an inlet where the sea comes up to a river. There's a long stretch of narrow beach there, and the hard sand near the water's edge was all churned up with the hoofprints of a galloping horse. The rest of the beach was full of the prints of the gauchos' horses but none of them had come down to the water's edge. You could see that the prints were distinct from the rest, big ones.'

'Has Serafin ever seen him?'

'Old Serafin! So he says, but that old one sees many things that others don't see so who's to know whether it's true or not. If anyone could catch the sand stallion, he could, and yet he never has.'

Aurelio had to acknowledge the truth of this last statement but, all the same, he fell to musing over what the shepherd had told him.

'And where is this beach where the stallion was seen going into the water?'

'You must ride south-east for at least half a day. Follow

the coast and eventually you'll come to the river's mouth. There you'll find the beach.'

'But couldn't the horse swim across the river?'

'No. It's far too wide there. It's more like a big bay. To find the river itself would take another afternoon's riding almost, following the beach. A horse entering the water there would surely be drowned. It's only a tale.'

Aurelio wondered, but of one thing he was determined. Legend or not, he would search for the sand stallion and if he did find it he would not return to the pampa until he had caught and tamed it and could take it back to Santa Clara as a gift for the major-domo.

II

By the time Aurelio was strong enough to get up on a horse again it was almost spring. His ribs were still strapped up in the woman's primitive bandages and he could not yet move with ease, but he was sick of his enforced idleness in the shepherd's house and, like a captive bird, longed for freedom.

The landscape was grey. The autumn mists had become thick Atlantic fogs which even the strong winds which blew in from the coast could hardly move. It rained often and Aurelio wondered if the sun ever shone on this God-forsaken part of the world.

His horses were wild and almost uncontrollable, having spent all the time of Aurelio's illness in hobbled freedom with no man to molest them. It took him a whole morning to find them all. They had wandered far in search of the mean fodder which the land provided and, had they not been hobbled, it would have been a difficult task to catch them. It was then that he longed for old Mouse, incapable of the smallest buck or twist, for his ribs were in no condition to endure the shaking that the colts would give them as soon as he was on their backs.

When he told the shepherd of his intention to search for the sand stallion, the man stared at him incredulously.

'You must be mad!' he exclaimed. 'It might take you months to even catch a glimpse of him—assuming that he exists, which I doubt—and meanwhile you'll freeze and die. I doubt that you're accustomed to such weather as this.'

'I can accustom myself to anything,' replied Aurelio, his self-confidence fully restored. 'I've taken advantage of your hospitality for long enough and now I must go.'

'Then go back to the pampa and don't be a fool.'

'Not until I've found the stallion. When I return to the pampa I intend to take him with me.'

'Fool!' reiterated the shepherd. 'But do as you please.'

The woman gave him a wool-lined jacket to wear beneath his poncho and the man a hunk of cured beef. 'The hunting is poor here,' he said. 'You'll go back to the pampa a lot thinner than when you left it.'

Aurelio thanked them again for their kindness and then, riding Lucero, he was on his way. His heart was light in spite of the wind and the rain that sprayed finely into his face. Instinct told him that the stallion existed and that he would find it.

He rode as the shepherd had directed him and as he neared the sea the rain had a salty flavour and was icy on his cheeks. His horses went forward with lowered heads. At first the rain had run off them in rivulets but now they were so soaked that it clung to their hair, grown thick in the many months that they had dwelt in this cold, unfriendly land.

By the time he reached the coast Aurelio's whole body ached and he knew that for that day at least he could go no further. He searched about for some form of shelter, which was only to be had from a copse of westerly-inclined gorse bushes. He hobbled the horses, made himself as comfortable as possible—which was very little—and pulled from his saddle-bag the cured beef. As the shepherd had warned him, there was nothing to hunt.

By nightfall he wished he had listened to the shepherd and not set out on such a journey. He was cold and pain-filled and miserable, and the sound of the sea reminded him of the spirits of which all the gauchos were afraid. It was too damp to light a fire, even had he possessed the energy to search for fuel, and he spent best part of the long, cold night in wakefulness, when even the thought of capturing the legendary stallion could not comfort him.

The next morning he felt more cheerful. The fog had lifted considerably and although the skies were still gloomy, giving the impression that the landscape was as grey as they were, at least he could see where he was going and felt less oppressed by the atmosphere. The sea was a stormy black and the waves crashed on to the beach with a fury that startled the boy.

Surely no horse, however powerful, could swim through that sea and survive? He stared keenly into the distance but the mist was heavy over the sea and little was visible beyond a short distance. The waves seemed to meet the fog and gave the impression that beyond was the end of the world; nothingness.

Aurelio saddled a different horse and decided that morning to find the river mouth. He followed the beach and at times was almost blown off the animal's back by the fierce gusts of wind that had gathered speed and fury out in mid-Atlantic and came rushing into the coast to flatten everything in their path. The noise of the sea and the rushing wind began to unnerve the boy, used to the silence of the pampa, broken only by sweet birdsong in the daytime.

He tried to sing, recalling one or two ballads that he had heard when they were driving cattle and making up his own phrases when he could not remember the correct ones, but the wind whipped the words out of his mouth and he could not even hear them. So he gave up singing and rode on in dour silence.

Eventually he came to what seemed to be the mouth of the river. A torrent of ice-cold water came rushing to meet the waves and, where they met, the water was brown and murky. It lashed and writhed. The land was marshy and thick with rushes which stood up fine and straight in spite of the wind which blew against them. To find shelter he had to go inland a way and he was luckier than in his previous quest for he found a hollow underneath a jutting, centuries old sand-bank. The wind and the sea-spray could not enter and there he felt almost comfortable.

The hollow became his base. He spent the next few days collecting driftwood, which he hoped would eventually dry enough for burning; he was able to capture a couple of ducks quite easily for so unused were they to creatures other than themselves in that deserted terrain that they were almost curious about him, allowing him to approach, grab them and cut their throats all within a matter of seconds.

He allowed the horses to roam in search of grazing and, as he finished hobbling them and sent them off with a whack on the rump, he suddenly wished that one of them had been a mare. She would have been good bait for the stallion. Still, perhaps even the smell of the geldings would be enough to attract him, for surely there were no other horses in this part of the world and curiosity would bring him, assuming that he was flesh and not just of the spirit.

III

Dawn never came until the morning was already advanced, and the daylight lasted but a few hours. Aurelio used those precious hours every day to search the beach and surrounding countryside for hoofprints. The rest of the time he spent huddled up in his poncho, sleeping as much as he could to forget his discomfort, almost in hibernation.

Often he was ready to give up his quest, so hopeless did it seem and so miserable was he, but he remembered what he owed to the major-domo and stayed on. He had nowhere in particular to go, anyway, if he could not return to Santa Clara.

The loneliness made his imagination acute and often he thought he could see a white stallion among the mists and fogs, but he was accustomed to seeing mirages on the pampa and knew when his eyes were deceiving him.

But surely his ears could not deceive him also?

He awoke one morning to the sound of excitement among the horses which never strayed far from his fireside at night. There were grunts and whinnies and the striking of hooves on the ground. Had the stallion come at last to visit them? Surely there was no other explanation.

Swiftly, but with caution, Aurelio arose and went in search of the horses. The fog was there as usual, cutting visibility down to almost nil and making of every shape something strange and unearthly. As the vague outlines of the horses came into view, he counted them.

One over to the right, standing still and watchful; the bay, too, with a similar stance. Where was the little dun with the black legs? In a moment Aurelio caught sight of him. He, too, was motionless and was staring with pricked ears into the mist-bound distance. As the boy drew near, he saw that the dun was trembling.

In the next second a big shape reared up out of the mist and there was the stallion, whiter, far whiter than his surroundings, with blood-red eyes that made him think of the bull, muscles that bulged and hooves that struck the ground haughtily. Aurelio stepped back, startled and struck almost with a chill of fear. In the same instant the stallion was gone and the boy was left wondering if he had seen or only dreamed that he had seen.

But no, the reactions of his ponies proved that it was no dream. The stallion, in spite of his awesome, spirit-like appearance; in spite of his incredible whiteness and the blood-red eyes, was flesh as he was and therefore could be caught and tamed.

In a moment Aurelio had the hobbles off the dun and was on its back, following the direction taken by the stallion. There was no sight of him but the hoofprints in the damp, sandy earth were deep and distinct and easy to follow. They led, as the legend had caused him to suppose, down to the beach as far as the water's edge.

When he got there, there was no sight of the stallion and the rough waves were already beginning to wash at the hoofprints and erase them.

16 : An outlaw's story

Minutes went by as Aurelio watched the waves creeping up on the hoofprints. He was almost mesmerised by their unceasing, relentless motion. Then he stared into the fog-bound sea, wondering how it was that the stallion could disappear into it and not be drowned. He knew, now that he had seen the animal, that it was of flesh and blood. Therefore it could not vanish into the sea without there being some practical explanation.

He could see nothing but the fog that touched the water, unmoving and grey, and he shivered, for the wind blew strongly in from the Atlantic. The dun grew restless and pawed at the sand. The wind tangled its mane and blew the black hairs against the boy's face as he leaned forward on the horse's back, trying to peer through the fog.

He had to admit that the stallion had defeated him unless he could discover the reason for its ability to vanish in such a spirit-like manner. The only way to discover it was by following it into the sea. Aurelio shuddered. The almost black water was not inviting and looked treacherous. He knew how to swim, for his main delight in the summer weather had been bathing in the river near his home, but there was a great difference between that slow, marshy water and this turbulent darkness that swept over the sand, reaching for his pony's hooves.

Surely he would die of cold in that water or be swept away? But the same could be said of the stallion. Even a horse could only resist for so long before growing tired and cold, and yet the stallion had come from the water and returned to it for at least six years, if the shepherd were to be believed.

Hesitating no longer, Aurelio urged the pony into the water. Having come so far to find the stallion he could not lose him now. With courage he would solve the riddle, of this he was sure, and he forced the dun against its will into the waves, gritting his teeth against the unbearable coldness of the water, his lessons in endurance proving not to be in vain.

The pony struggled and resisted until, caught from

behind by the waves that receded swiftly from the shore, he was forced to go on. Then, with the courage of his race and the urgings of his master, he struck out towards the grey horizon, plunging and snorting, his eyes wild with fright.

Aurelio clung to the pony's mane with his hands and to his back with his knees. Never had he welded himself so closely to a horse as now and, as the water rose up to the gelding's withers, such a coldness came over him that soon he was unable to feel his legs at all, nor the body of the pony. He was swept from the dun's back and grabbed at its neck fiercely, his fingers locked together and frozen in that position.

He lost all count of time and direction, dragged through the sea by the struggling horse, and for a while he must have lost consciousness too. All he knew was that they were in the grip of a strong current, dragging them he knew not whither. To the stallion, he thought, To the stallion, and then the waves no longer crashed over his head and he thought of nothing.

His next awareness came when the dun was no longer swimming and seemed to have firm ground under its hooves once more. Aurelio was unable to release his fingers from their frozen grasp and he floated beside the pony until at last he could get a leg across its back again. Thus he remained, half on the pony and half in the water, until the waves suddenly receded and the dun brought him to shore.

The gelding stood still with drooping head, too exhausted even to shake the water from its body, and Aurelio slipped from its back, his fingers loosened at last, to fall unconscious to the ground.

II

Aurelio came to his senses aware of warmth and dryness, and a darkness that was broken by the flickering light of a fire. At first he thought he was in the shepherd's hut and all that had gone before was but a dream, but as his brain regained its clarity he dismissed the idea. He was lying on a sheepskin rug, a thick poncho over him, and the warmth of the two combined almost lulled him back into slumber, for he was thoroughly battered by his sojourn in the sea and had no energy for anything.

For a moment his eyes closed but they opened again sharply as a shadow fell over him. It was a gaucho by his dress, no doubt the owner of the place in which he rested. His beard was grey and his hair came down to his shoulders.

'Where am I?' said Aurelio.

'In your house,' replied the gaucho, which was his way of offering the boy his hospitality.

'But where did you find me? Did you bring me here?'

'I saw your horse and looked for you.'

'But where is this place? I don't recall having seen any homestead in these parts, except for the shepherd's, and that's a good journey from here.'

'I know him. No, you're nowhere near the shepherd's home, nor are you anywhere that you could imagine, though I can guess how you got here.'

The gaucho went over to the fire. A kettle hung over its flames from which gushed a volley of steam. Aurelio slowly sat up, pulling the poncho around him, and watched in silence while his host prepared a pot of maté. He was even more puzzled by the man's last words.

Now he was aware again of the sound of the sea, loud

and unceasing, which made him think that he must be somewhere along the shore still. The hut was very tiny and Aurelio was obviously lying on the gaucho's bed for there was no other in the room.

The gaucho brought the maté over to the boy and squatted down beside him. They shared it between them in silence. Aurelio's head was spinning with questions, so many that he did not know where to begin, while his companion's expression suggested that he was not thinking of anything at all.

But at last the gaucho spoke and his words, quiet and unexpected, were startling.

'You're on an island,' he said, 'an island that's not very far away from the beach. On a clear day it can be plainly seen but on a day like this no one would ever guess of its existence. If you see it from a distance, it looks as though it's part of the mainland. The fact is that this part of the world is the most deserted on God's earth. No one ever comes this way and, should they do so, they don't stay long enough to discover its secrets.'

'But the shepherd?' broke in Aurelio.

'The shepherd has only been in these parts once and it was on a day as grey as this one. He thinks I live inland. No one knows about this little rancho of mine except you and the stallion.'

'The stallion!'

'Yes. The one you were undoubtedly chasing. What else would have caused you to launch yourself into the sea like a madman? Why else would you be in these parts?'

Aurelio explained what had happened and his companion listened with nodding head, without interrupting.

'You have courage at least,' was his only comment

when the boy had finished.

'And the stallion?' said Aurelio eagerly. 'Was I right? Did I follow him here? Is this where he comes?'

'And if it is?'

'Well . . .' He paused, for a thought had struck him. 'I suppose he belongs to you?'

The gaucho shook his head.

'We share the island, that's all. He doesn't molest me and I don't molest him.'

'You mean you've never tried to catch him?'

The incredulity in his voice amused the gaucho.

'Why should I? We're a pair of recluses who happen to have found refuge from the world in the same place. It may not be the most comfortable, nor the most accommodating, but neither of us wanted to be disturbed by men and this is about the only place that, until your arrival, men have never come to.'

The gaucho brewed another pot of maté and when he had once again squatted down beside the mystified boy he told him one of the strangest stories that he had ever heard and one that, in all places, he had least expected to hear.

'I'm an outlaw,' he began, 'a deserter from the army. You don't know what the army's like and I hope you'll never have cause to. It's a long time ago now that I was as free as any man under the sun. One day I went to a race meeting and, for a reason I don't even remember now, I got into a fight with another gaucho. I was a hot-blooded fellow in those days and wouldn't take an insult from anybody, and he was a bad one who would rather use a knife than words to settle his quarrels. It's a bad thing to start a fight but, if a man pulls a knife at you, what can you do? I killed him, without ever meaning to, and there were witnesses in plenty to prove that it was self-defence.'

He snorted, even now angry at the memory of that long-ago day.

'It was obvious that the army was short of men—which doesn't surprise me as no-one in their right senses would volunteer—and the judge didn't even listen to my argument. Twenty-five years was the sentence, and a staking-out besides. I would have killed that judge with pleasure, could I have got my hands on him.'

The gaucho rambled on for a long time about his life in the army, full of woes and injustice, hunger and pain, and Aurelio listened with his eyes shut. He had snuggled back under the poncho and felt warm and dreamy. The sea still roared outside the hut but he hardly heard it. He almost fell asleep and the voice of his companion, silent for too long to be anything less than voluble, was lulling him slowly into that state.

Was it instinct that suddenly jerked him into wakefulness, that made him all at once take notice, when the gaucho brought a companion into his story whose woes were even greater than his own? A young man he was, at least twenty years the story-teller's junior, and he was dragged into the outpost more dead than alive, having suffered at the hands of a justice of peace, much as had the former.

'They said he was a terrible criminal,' recalled Aurelio's host, 'but all gauchos are criminals even before we've committed a crime. This one was supposed to have kidnapped the daughter of a rich man and then to have murdered her, but it was just an excuse to bring the army up to strength, for the Indians were a lot stronger than we were.'

'What happened to him?' asked Aurelio, an eager listener once more.

'I had been wounded in a battle against the Indians, which kept me around the fort for a while, so I looked after him until he was able to look after himself, which is how we became companions. Mind you, he made himself popular with most of the men because he was a bit of a poet and, heaven knows, we all needed a few songs to cheer us up. We were all desperate men, with hardly a meal a day and even the horses starving.

'Anyway, this one was determined to escape just as soon as he could, for all that he could hardly stand on his feet. I held him back for a while—he would never have succeeded otherwise—and then we decided to escape together. There was only one place we could go to until our desertion should be forgotten, and that was to the Indians.'

The gaucho paused, no doubt remembering too vividly the past that this boy had unexpectedly caused him to conjure up.

'Go on,' said Aurelio impatiently. 'What happened next?'

'Oh, we escaped and the Indians accepted us in their way, which wasn't a friendly one. But at least they allowed us to live on their lands without molesting us, which was all we wanted. At least, it was all I wanted. I had no one to go back to and it was all the same to me if I lived in one place or another. But for my companion it was different.

'The woman he was supposed to have kidnapped was in reality his wife. They had run away together and married in spite of her father, who had tried to prevent them. But she died, after giving birth to a son, and it was only a few days afterwards that he was captured by the men the girl's father had paid to search for them. It would seem that the pair had been on the run in all the short time they were married, trying to escape their pursuers. Perhaps if they hadn't stopped at that township they might have eventually escaped them.

'The girl's father was a powerful man, very rich, and when he learned that his daughter was dead his rage was insatiable. My friend refused to tell him where the baby was. Whether he ever found out, I wouldn't know. So, you see, he had to get back to find his son, regardless of the danger involved.'

'But he never did?' suddenly broke in Aurelio.

'How did you know?'

Aurelio was silent and the man went on, 'No, he didn't fulfil his intention for the simple reason that a plague broke out among the Indians. They died at a terrible rate, almost the whole tribe was wiped out, and my companion wasn't spared either. I nursed him as best I could for several days but it was no good. Before he died he gave me the medallion that he wore. It had belonged to his wife. He was delirious most of the time but I understood that he wanted me to find his son and give it to him. I still have it.

'I buried him as best I could and then I left that place, before the plague got at me, too. I'd already survived it once as a child, which was probably why I escaped this time, too. For a while I tried to find the boy but he had never told me the name of the place, and then one day I learned that the army was after me again. The father of my friend's wife had been informed of our desertion and he was determined to track us down. It seemed that not only one daughter had run away from him, but two. The second was presumably caring for the baby.

'Anyway, I tired of being constantly hounded from place to place, and eventually I got down to this part of the world, found it deserted and decided to stop here. I discovered this island, quite by accident, and it suits me perfectly. Now and again I leave it to buy the few things that I need. I've lost count of the years I've been here. The past all seems like a dream. The present suits me well enough. I've a horse of my own and the stallion for company. He's been coming here on and off for a long time too.'

He went on to describe to Aurelio how one dark day the stallion had come up from the sea, unbelievably white, unbelievably beautiful, and he had hidden in his hut at first, believing him to be a spirit.

'But when he proved himself to be a horse I stopped hiding and went about my life as usual. It's a small island but big enough for the pair of us. Tomorrow I'll show it to you.'

His tale finished, the old gaucho got up and went to tend the fire. He sat staring into the curling smoke and said no more to the boy. Perhaps he was remembering the past again, things he had not spoken out loud. For a while Aurelio watched him, his heart and mind in turmoil, but then the warmth and comfort overcame him in his weariness and he once again relapsed into sleep.

17 : The Indian's way

The following morning, after a night restless with dreams
and emotions, Aurelio told the grey-bearded gaucho his
own story. There was a long silence when he finished and
then the man suddenly pulled a small leather bag from
under his belt and tipped its contents into his hand. There

were several coins of copper and silver and a golden medallion with a fine, crumpled chain. With rough fingers the gaucho took hold of the delicate object and handed it over to Aurelio.

'Then this must be yours,' he said simply. 'I'm glad that I've been able to fulfill my friend's request.'

Almost with awe, Aurelio fingered the medallion which had belonged first to his mother and then to his father. On its face was the figure of the Virgin with a tiny child in her arms. He turned it over and saw written the name 'Barbara' and underneath the date of her birth thirty-three years earlier. So at last he had reached the end of his quest for his father, a strange place in which to do so, a fog-bound island off the Atlantic coast.

The gaucho left him to ponder over these things and went outside. His first sight was of the three horses, his own, the boy's and the stallion, grazing together off the rough bit of fodder the island afforded. All three looked up at him with pricked ears, then after a few seconds returned to their search. None was afraid.

The gaucho returned to the hut. Aurelio was still turning the medallion over in his hands, lost in his thoughts, so much so that he jumped when at last the former spoke.

'God has his own ways of leading a man to his goal. It must be that he meant the stallion to be yours, for it was by following him here that you found what you were seeking. Come outside and you'll see him.'

The boy sprang up but stopped as the gaucho lifted his hand peremptorily.

'Quietly. Slowly. Remember, he's as nervous as the wind.'

Aurelio stood silently beside the gaucho in the doorway of the hut and now the medallion in his hand was forgotten as he looked so closely upon the beautiful stallion.

The albino was in his twelfth year now and his body had grown powerfully heavy. Muscles bulged under the thick hair that coated him, his forelock almost hid his eyes, while his tail was so long that it almost touched the ground. Aurelio noticed that a twig was caught up in it. He had never seen so magnificent an animal and even now had to wonder if this were not all a dream, in spite of the wind that blustered round them, in spite of the golden piece growing warm in his grasp.

The stallion looked up at the boy, his gaze haughty even in wariness. He tossed his head and whickered and began to move away. He was no longer afraid of man but could not trust him.

'He knows you don't belong here,' said the gaucho.

'If I could only capture him . . .'

The gaucho was shaking his head.

'No one can capture him,' he said. 'You must gain his trust and hope that he will surrender himself to you. For now, it's best to take no notice of him. I'll show you what there is of the island. Pretend in the meanwhile that the stallion doesn't exist.'

They mounted their horses and rode from one end of the island to the other, a distance of about a mile. The wind blustered about them, salty and damp, and they rode with bowed heads and hunched shoulders. Aurelio's teeth were chattering and he wondered how his companion could possibly endure such a climate year after year. The mist was thinner that morning and it was possible to see the mainland as a vague shadow beyond the dark, undulating waves.

Driftwood and weeds cluttered the island and a colony of gulls hardly disturbed themselves as the horsemen approached. Aurelio became aware that the white stallion was following them.

'Don't look round,' the old gaucho warned him, divining his desire. 'Let him get to know you in his own way. Remember, this is his island and mine.'

It was difficult to resist the temptation but Aurelio obeyed. They rode their horses slowly about the whole island and the stallion followed, as shy and as curious as a bird. Aurelio forgot the bitterness in the wind, hot with excitement.

He wondered at his companion's words, doubting the wisdom of them. How could anyone ever gain the trust of such an animal? How could it, of its own accord, surrender itself to him? The only way to own him was by capturing him and dominating him the way the gauchos had shown him. This old man was a bit queer in the head, which was hardly surprising with the life he led. He had come to think of the horse as a person, which explained why he spoke as he did.

Again the gaucho seemed to guess his thoughts.

'You must be patient,' he suddenly said. 'Very patient. Such an animal as this was never won in a day.'

II

Aurelio was patient. He whiled away the hours listening to the old man's stories, asking him questions about his father and also about the horse. While the wind howled and the waves crashed, he learned a good deal about the former but was left in doubt about the stallion. He knew of only one way to dominate a horse. It was a hard way for him, still not perfectly skilled in equestrian arts, but he felt that sheer pig-headedness would help him to victory in the end, just as it had with Bicho.

When his host told him that there was another way, when he spoke of gentling the horse instead of breaking him, he was puzzled and disbelieving. And even greater was his disbelief when the gaucho said that it was an art the Indians practised. The Indians were feared all over the land for their barbarous customs and cruelties. How could they be gentle with a horse?

The gaucho explained how he had seen them still the tossings of the wildest stallion by breathing into its nostrils. It was a common custom for them to 'talk' to their horses in this way. They would copy the sounds that the horses made, soft grunts and whickerings which the animals seemed to understand, for they would almost immediately lose their fear and allow a man on their backs with hardly a tremble.

'You haven't the strength to beat that stallion into submission,' he said to Aurelio. 'And I'm too old. You must try the Indian's way, even though you don't believe in it.'

Aurelio tried.

Whenever the horse was near he would talk to it as gently as he could. The stallion would watch him with pricked ears and after a while the suspicion would die out of his expression, replaced by curiosity. Never once did Aurelio try to approach the horse, held back by the gaucho's warnings. He was as still as a thistle when the wind has dropped. Only his voice went on and on, murmuring soft words and nonsense until it seemed as though the stallion was growing to like the sound of it.

He was beginning to think that he was being accepted, and rejoicing in the fact with his companion, when the stallion disappeared. For a week he kept away from the island and Aurelio was in despair, first with the horse and then with the weather which was depressing in the extreme.

'Be patient,' the old man continued to counsel him. 'The stallion will come back and he won't have forgotten you,' but he was used to whiling away his life in this bleak loneliness. It was harder for a lad of fourteen, used to blue skies and sunshine and the wide, green pampa.

The stallion returned and his curiosity was as great as ever. He hung about the hut with the two geldings, watching the boy, listening to him, unable to connect him with the savage, shrieking gauchos that had tormented and terrified him so long ago. There was a rhythm in the soft voice that was pleasant to his ears; no threat in the comparatively small and motionless figure; and Aurelio saw that it was as the gaucho had promised him. The stallion lost his caution and had no fear of him.

Following the old man's advice, realising now that the recluse was not so crazy as he seemed, Aurelio refrained from touching the horse. He let the stallion see how he fondled his own pony and made advances to the old gaucho's mount also. The albino saw that neither were afraid and even welcomed the boy's attentions. He trembled when the boy mounted his pony and circled him about, calmly, silently, but his ears were pricked and it seemed to Aurelio that the animal brain was digesting the information he was trying to impart.

Though at times he was impatient, wearying of never attaining his desire, that of mounting the beautiful horse he had set his heart on, he was glad too, that the gaucho had shown him this other way of taming the animal. Underneath the callous exterior that the last two years had formed in self-protection, there was still that sensitive boy who enjoyed the sound of bird song and pleasured in the delicate pattern of a rose. To feel that proud animal's body beneath him would be as gratifying as having a skylark perched on his fingers. Could such wildness be subdued? Could so great a confidence grow out of such mistrust?

'When can I try to touch him?' he constantly asked of his host and, after many times replying, 'Not yet, not yet,' the old gaucho one day said, 'You'll know when the moment is right. Until you know, it will be too soon.'

So Aurelio curbed his impatient heart and waited. Spring flowers were pushing themselves up through the few earthly patches on the isand, and there was even a touch of sunshine now and again to break the dark monotony of the days. The stallion came and went and many a time Aurelio would have followed him, weary of the island, longing for the grasslands that seemed but a dream in such a place as this. He tired of the stale, roughly cured meat that was all he lived on, interspersed occasionally with the tough flesh of a gull. He tired of the sound of the sea, the sound of the wind, even of the gaucho who spent long hours in silence and seemed to forget that the boy existed.

After yet another long stay away, Aurelio was determined to make the stallion his. He longed for the albino's return and when eventually the horse came plunging up through the waves one day, the long mane streaming water, his heart leapt with excitement. This was the moment, he was sure.

He waited just a few yards off, watching while the stallion shook off the water from his heavy body. As the albino came up the short stretch of beach, Aurelio went forward to meet him, arms outstretched, voice suddenly steady and certain.

'Come, beautiful one. You belong to me. You know it already. Come. Come.'

And the stallion came, blowing through his pink nostrils, lowering his head and touching the boy's hands with his wet muzzle. Aurelio's hand smoothed its way up the sea-soaked head, touching the jaw, the throat and then that powerful neck, and the stallion was still, accepting his touch, blowing through his nostrils, but gently, his breath warm on the frozen hand.

For several minutes they stood together thus, the stallion warming the boy with his closeness. Aurelio's sense of triumph was tinged with dread. Still he had not mounted the horse and was almost afraid to do so. The moment was too wonderful to lose. If the horse rejected him he would come no more to the island and Aurelio would never have a second chance to gain his confidence. At the same time he knew he must go ahead, now, while the horse was consenting. He must be more gentle than the summer wind, but he must be determined.

Summoning all his courage, Aurelio smoothed his way along the stallion's flank. The horse began to jerk his head slightly, as if sensing the boy's inner turmoil, and even as he danced away from him Aurelio was on his back. The stallion jumped, reared slightly and kicked out with his hind legs. But it was a small protest, one that Aurelio could sit out easily without even clinging, and then the stallion was still. He quivered from withers to rump, trust in the boy and suddenly remembered fears conflicting. But there was no pain, no terrifying noise, no force, and the trembling died away.

Aurelio forced words from his dry throat, gentle, meaningless words that caused the stallion to prick his ears again and turn them back to catch the sounds. Then he smoothed his hands over the albino's neck, and the horse began to move.

He pranced with his high, proud gait, head tossing, nostrils distended, tail lifted, and the boy could hardly believe that it was a horse he rode. He felt like a god, striding a cloud, the rough winds blustering about him, and he let the stallion take him where he would, forgetting the existence of everything, even of himself.

He did not see the old gaucho, watching him from the doorway of the hut, and he was startled back into himself again only when the stallion danced through the gull colony and sent the birds crying up on either side of them. Aurelio laughed, the horse snorted, and the gulls wheeled about their heads, scolding loudly.

18 : The return

When Aurelio and the albino stallion found themselves
in the land of the ombu-tree once again, summer lay
heavily over the pampa. The thistles were dry and
crackling in the breeze, the ground was hard and taut as a
drum-skin. Aurelio felt the music in the hoof-beats of his

little troup of horses, cantering in solitary state across the
deserted plain. He was riding the albino, the sand
stallion, and he was a king in spite of his stained and dirty
clothes and the bare toes that gripped the stirrups.

Joy overcame his pride as his eyes were filled with the
sights that had grown so dear to him, the withered grass
and bracken, the flocks of birds making dancing dark
patches in its yellowness, the shining mirage on the
horizon of trees and houses. Through his own joy he
recognised a stirring in the stallion, too; the increased
effortlessness of his pace, the constantly pricked ears and
widened nostrils. Surely these were signs of the stallion's
gladness to be back in the land that God had given to the
gaucho and his ponies?

Aurelio and the stallion had come to know each other
well in the few weeks that they had travelled together.
From their long association on the island, Aurelio's heart
had expanded into love for this still wild creature that
had come to put its trust in him.

When they halted for the night and the horses grazed
together not far from Aurelio's resting place, hobbled
except for the stallion, there were times when he had to
believe that it was all a dream and that he would wake
up and find the albino gone. He disdained haltering the
legs of this wild one, for still he felt he had no right to
call the stallion his. If one day it chose to desert him,
called again to the liberty it had forsaken, Aurelio knew
that greater than regret and sorrow would be the privi-
leged memory of having once ridden him and exercised
a calming influence over him.

Sometimes he almost wanted him to go, feeling that he
was not entitled to cling to him as a piece of personal
property, and when the stallion stayed, in spite of the

winds and the smells and the sounds that teased him, Aurelio's love for him grew greater.

He did not know why the stallion stayed. One night, when the moon was so bright that he could not sleep, he watched the albino, whiter than ever in the silver-lit darkness. His head and shoulders comfortably resting against the saddle, his fingers absently twisting the gold medallion about his neck, he saw how the stallion sought out the different scents, body alternately taut or quivering, and never had he realised until that moment how wild he really was, forgetful now of the boy who held sway over his instincts. Why did he not go? Why did he stay when every breath of wind tormented him?

He wanted him to go, to be free, galloping tracelessly over the land that belonged to him. His conscience was as heavy as his heart was full for, with Indian wile, he had made this essentially free creature his slave.

It was in one of these pensive moments that Aurelio remembered the vow he had made in the shepherd's hut, to return to the pampa only when he could bring back the sand stallion as a gift for the major-domo. He had no right to give this horse to another person, any more than he had the right to take it for himself. But a vow was a vow and he could not escape it.

In spite of this, he smiled when he remembered Serafin, who had always been around to give advice when it was needed and to mock at him when he grew presumptuous. Surely there was no better person to whom he could give the stallion? He was understanding, for all that he was rough, and cared well for his favourite mounts.

Remembering, Aurelio knew that he still wanted to take the stallion to him for all that he ached to think of parting with the horse. How else could he show the major-domo that he was grateful for all that he had done? He knew that the gaucho wanted no thanks for having saved his life but he knew, too, that only by sacrificing something dear of his own could he ever repay him.

In the days that were left to them Aurelio greatly cherished the white stallion. He continued to fill the sharply pricked ears with the sound of his voice; he even learned—shyly at first—to breathe into the stallion's big nostrils, wondering if the animal way of communicating would bring them closer.

The stallion was still his powerful, haughty self, but the boy with his gentleness had reached the docility that was also within him. Essentially a gregarious animal, after his long isolation the undemanding friendship the boy offered him was all he needed to subdue his mistrust of mankind and sublimate his instinctive fear. He did not even quiver when the boy lightly strode him, knowing that no harm would come from him, and he had no sense of being captive for he had come of his own accord. Though the winds spoke of space and liberty, the stallion lacked neither. He rejoiced in the early summer smells and he rejoiced in his companion.

Aurelio felt the joy that was in the stallion and because of his intentions his heart was sometimes heavy. Was he not betraying the stallion, taking him to Santa Clara?

II

The young son of one of the gauchos who worked at Santa Clara was whiling away the afternoon standing on his pony's back and watching the horizon. Both boy and pony had been as still as a reed on a windless day for a long time. The pony was asleep but its ears automatically twitched as the sound of hurrying hooves reached them. The boy saw the slight movement and continued his watch with more emotion. Something, or someone, was coming, though not yet in sight, and he waited until a few specks appeared on the yellow horizon. Then he thumped into the saddle by opening his legs, waking the pony with a start, and dashed back to the ranch house, calling to its owner.

'Someone's coming, Don Jacinto. Someone's coming. A man with four horses, Don Jacinto.'

The scattering of dogs began to bark, a couple of tethered horses moved restlessly, but Don Jacinto was asleep and so profoundly that even the three flies crawling about his face did not disturb him.

Action was the only antidote to the tedious afternoon and the boy raced off to where the gauchos were herding, followed by a crowd of dogs. The boy's father told the major-domo and Serafin left someone else in charge, took a fresh horse and returned to the estancia to await the traveller. It was probably a gaucho looking for work and Don Jacinto would be annoyed if woken for such a detail.

Thus it was that when Aurelio arrived there was none but the major-domo to greet him. He stopped the stallion at a hundred yards from the gate-posts—the only sign that suggested that here the pampa stopped for a while and civilisation began—too shy now to approach the man he had longed to see. He was sure that the gaucho would ridicule him for his presumption in taking up his last-flung challenge and, worse still, succeeding.

The major-domo's face was impassive but it was he who urged his own splendid horse forward and rode to greet the returning boy.

He halted a length's distance away and sat back in the saddle to admire the stallion. The albino grew nervous at the man's proximity. He pawed the ground and tossed his head, his anxious hooves beginning to dance, but Aurelio uttered a few soft words and stilled him.

'Well,' said the major-domo at last. 'You've come back. I thought you'd forgotten us.'

There were so many things that Aurelio wanted to say but it was not the right moment for any of them. So he remained silent, gazing down at the horse's withers, not daring to meet the other's eyes for fear he should not find in them the welcome he needed.

'I see that you've come back with a new horse.' The voice was still cold.

'It's the sand stallion. You told me to look for him. That's why I've been away so long.'

There was a hint of anger in the boy's voice, to disguise his terrible disappointment at Serafin's reception of him.

'So you return more gaucho than all of us! Congratulations!'

'It's for you,' suddenly burst out Aurelio. 'For the one that died. I only wanted to find him for you.'

Suddenly the gaucho was laughing and holding out his arms to the boy. He kneed his horse close and was hugging him, almost unsaddling him as the stallion grew afraid again and jerked away.

'Get down from there,' shouted the major-domo, 'so I can see if you've grown or not. It's probably only the horse that makes you look like a man.'

They dismounted simultaneously and the man's arms were round the boy again, holding him in close embrace. His voice was gruff as he spoke once more.

'I haven't slept a peaceful night since I left you with

the shepherd. I knew what you'd be up to.'

Aurelio grinned and, looking up at the major-domo's expressive face, he now understood something that had been puzzling him ever since he had discovered the island and, with it, the end of his father's story. It had left him almost unmoved—the nearness of the stallion had excited him far more—and this was strange, for all his lifetime he had wanted to know who his father was.

With Serafin's arm about his shoulder, the truth at last was plain. Guiding, mocking, caring, the major-domo had been in these last two years as much his father as any man could be. The other, always a shadowy figure, faded into non-existence beside him. He had pursued a dream and found a father.

All this he tried to explain to the major-domo but his enthusiastic words came out in such a muddle and at such a spate that the gaucho could make little sense of them. While Aurelio rushed on he was watching the stallion. He saw how the albino's gaze rested on the boy, the ears flicking with the changes in his voice, and there was something in the look that he recognised. There was no wildness, no mistrust. It was questioning, eager, expectant; the look that he had often found in the eyes of his own favourite horse.

He had to wonder how Aurelio could dominate this powerful animal, so much larger than the average pony and strong in his years, and he had to conclude that no physical force had wrought from the horse his wildness.

At last he interrupted the boy, waving aside his voluble explanations.

'Is that horse really broken? Can anyone ride him, or is it just your magic touch that controls him?'

The old irony was in his words but Aurelio was no

longer so sensitive to it, still flushed with the excitement of his discovery.

'I don't know. He answers well enough to heel and rein but I don't know how he'll behave with another person.'

'Can I try him?'

'He's yours,' said Aurelio, but he could not keep a certain anxiety from his voice.

He wanted to tell the gaucho to be gentle, to use no whip or spurs, but he could not say such things to the major-domo. Besides, the horse was his now and he could do with it as he liked.

He stood at the albino's head while the gaucho approached and his confidence was somewhat restored as he saw how Serafin first smoothed his hand along the stallion's restless neck and spoke softly to him. He gathered up the reins in a nonchalant manner and in a second was in the saddle, relaxed but vigilant. The albino tossed his head and flattened his ears but the boy at his head kept him from alarm.

'Let him go,' said the gaucho. 'Let's see how he runs.'

Aurelio took his hand from the bridle. Serafin touched the stallion's flanks slightly with his spurs. The horse reared, pawed the air, then sprang into a gallop. He ran with a grace that was beautiful to behold and he ran without fear.

The gaucho gave him his head and soon Aurelio was left alone at the gate-posts, with only the major-domo's horse for company. There was a strange feeling in his heart, both of joy and sadness. He could never feel again that the stallion belonged to him.

After a while the major-domo returned. The stallion was cantering now, head held high, tail floating out behind him in the breeze. The gaucho was so much a part of the horse, his own body moving in exact relativity with that of the animal, that even Aurelio had to admit that they belonged together.

Serafin sprang from the saddle even before the stallion had drawn to a halt. He dropped the reins into Aurelio's hands and grinned at him.

'What a ride! As tame as a lamb! I thought you said this was the sand stallion. Here, take him. He's yours. We both lost a horse that day, remember.'

Aurelio mounted the stallion again who was blowing and shaking his head, his eager hooves still printing the grass. Serafin was up on his own horse beside them.

'You'd better collect your other horses. There's some herding to be done and I've wasted enough of the afternoon already.'

Aurelio rode back for Lucero and the two geldings who snatched at the grass while they waited for him. He did not know what to make of the gaucho's words. Was Serafin doing him a favour, or did he really disparage the gift?

As he returned to the rancho, he recognised one of the horses half-dozing in the nearby corral. Surely that mealy-coloured creature with the swollen joints and the rheumy eyes was his old Mouse? His heart flooded with affection at the sight of him and suddenly he remembered how he had first ridden up to Santa Clara on the feeble animal. He had learned a lot since that long-ago day, and now he rode a full-blooded stallion that many a man had wanted to possess.

He would have gone up to the horse and called to him but Serafin was growing impatient. He had no time for such an overflow of sentiment and had wasted a lot already that afternoon.

'Come on!' he cried. 'Shake up that bag of bones you're riding!'

'But don't you want him?' answered Aurelio, disappointment in his voice. 'I brought him for you. I only went after him for you.'

The major-domo shook his head.

'I've had my share of beautiful horses. You deserve him. Don't be so anxious to give him away.'

He spurred his mount and galloped off in the direction of the herders, looking back at Aurelio and waving at him to follow.

He shouted, 'Let him teach you how to ride, boy. He'll make a gaucho of you yet.'

The stallion was only waiting for Aurelio to give him his head. He flung himself after the retreating figures and was soon abreast of them. The gaucho shouted and spurred his horse faster. Aurelio was taunted by his teasing to do the same and soon both horses were stretched out in headlong gallop, their riders encouraging them with yells of delight.

Old Mouse in the corral pricked his ears, disturbed by the music of their hooves. Then he returned to his dozing in the sunshine, which was all he was good for now.

Knight has a whole range of paperbacks for boys and girls, from mystery, adventure and crime to fantasy, animal stories and factual books on sport and other activities for the holidays.

If you've enjoyed STALLION OF THE SANDS, why not have a look at some of our other paperbacks on sale? You will see them displayed in your local booksellers. Meanwhile, on the pages following, you will see some of our suggestions for novels that we think will give you an idea of the range that is available in Knight—the brightest and best in children's paperbacks.

KATHLEEN FIDLER

Haki the Shetland Pony

This is the story of Adam Cromarty and his Shetland colt Haki. Haki was born on Adam's father's croft, and was given to Adam for his own. A strong sympathy grew up between them, and Adam spent a great deal of time and trouble on Haki's training.

But the day came when Adam was told the pony must be sold. And sold he was—to a circus . . .

ROY BROWN

A Flight of Sparrows

A tense, gripping story about life on the run in London's East End.

That's the lot of Scobie, Keith, young Sprog, the strange Boy and his dog. Scobie, already a young criminal, has escaped from an approved school, taking Keith with him. He is cunning, even violent, and his savage plans show utter contempt for the law and even for his companions.

Keith realises he must escape again—this time from Scobie.

IVAN SOUTHALL

Seventeen Seconds

'. . . There is a little part that is always alive. That's the bomb fuse . . . If anything goes wrong, you'll hear the fuse run. It's a time clock. You've got anything up to seventeen seconds. When you hear that fuse run . . . jump clean over ten-foot walls like they weren't there . . . you're four hundred yards away or else.'

The true, heroic story of John Stuart Mould and Hugh Syme, Australians who volunteered for mine-disposal work in Britain during World War II, and their many brushes with death. To them was given the task of dismantling the deadly acoustic mines . . . with seventeen seconds to blast-off if any false move was made.

L. H. EVERS

The Racketty Street Gang

Raquetier Street, disreputable and exciting, runs along Sydney's harbour. Here Anton, a recent immigrant to Australia, joins up with the adventure-loving Racketty Street Gang. Soon the boys are faced with mystery in a boatyard closely guarded by the cruel Tommo. In trying to unravel that mystery, the gang discovers that the very life of Anton's father is at stake—as well as their own!

Action and Excitement for Older Readers

KATHLEEN FIDLER
☐ 16947 8   Haki, the Shetland Pony   45P

ROY BROWN
☐ 18739 5   A Flight of Sparrows   60p

IVAN SOUTHALL
☐ 20132 0   Seventeen Seconds   60p

L. H. EVERS
☐ 16744 0   The Racketty Street Gang   60p

All these books are available at your local bookshop or newsagent, or can be ordered direct from the publisher. Just tick the titles you want and fill in the form below.

Prices and availability subject to change without notice.

KNIGHT BOOKS, P.O. Box 11, Falmouth, Cornwall.

Please send cheque or postal order, and allow the following for postage and packing:

U.K.—One book 19p plus 9p per copy for each additional book ordered, up to a maximum of 73p.

B.F.P.O. and EIRE—19p for the first book plus 9p per copy for the next 6 books, thereafter 3p per book.

OTHER OVERSEAS CUSTOMERS—20p for the first book and 10p per copy for each additional book.

Name...

Address ....

....